RARER THAN GOLD

A CHANCE INQUIRY BOOK 2

HOLLY NEWMAN

OLIVER
HEBER
BOOKS

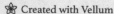 Created with Vellum

1

"Come in," called out Sir James Branstoke at the light knock on the estate room door. He exchanged puzzled looks with his new bride, Lady Cecilia Haukstrom Waddley Branstoke, at the interruption. They had adjourned to the estate room after breakfast and were seated across from each other, discussing the improvements necessary to bring Summerworth Park back to a profitable state.

As far as their friends in London knew, they'd left on their honeymoon trip to the highlands immediately following their wedding at one of the Wren chapels in London four weeks ago. Instead, they'd traveled down to Kent, south of Maidstone, to Summerworth Park, an estate at the edge of the South Downs that Sir James recently purchased from his cousin, the new Earl of Morchant.

The earl's elder brother and father, between them, had devastated the family fortune, and it was the task of the second son, now Earl, to set the family fortunes to right as best he might do in order to provide for his orphaned twin half-sisters, Eugenia and Augusta. The first thing he did was find purchasers for his unentailed properties. The Summerworth Park Georgian manor and properties came to him from his mother. As Sir James' mother and his mother had been sisters, he thought it fitting that the property stay within his family, so he'd approached James to buy the estate.

Sir James had been happy to acquire the property, for he had fond memories of visiting the estate as a child. Unfortunately, the years and the deprivations of the old earl had seen the estate fall into disrepair. He now understood why his cousin had sold it to him for a song! Luckily, his new wife had been delighted with the opportunity and the challenge of bringing the estate around, and it was she who decided she'd rather spend time on the estate versus traveling north for a honeymoon. There would be other occasions for trips.

He enjoyed sitting in the estate room with his new bride in the mornings. While he projected an image of a gentleman unruffled and perpetually at his leisure, this was the first time in a long while that he felt as relaxed as his public mien suggested.

As Cecilia looked at her writing notes, her pale blond hair glowed golden in the morning sun streaming into the room. She was a prize he'd never thought to have, a jewel rarer than gold, a woman of intellect, humor, determination, loyalty, and love.

And he owned he would never have done more than indulged in a trifling flirt with her if she hadn't— quite unwittingly—snubbed him at Lady Amblethorp's musicale, and he, like a hound to a scent, had become determined to find out why. He smiled wryly at the merry—and sometimes frightening— chase she'd led him on.

"Excuse me, Sir James, your ladyship," said Coggins, the Summerworth Park butler, "this letter just came for you from Folkestone."

"Ah, good, Coggins," James said, standing up and

extending his hand to take the letter from the silver tray the butler carried.

Cecilia looked up at her husband. "Do you think it is in response to those inquiries you sent out?" she asked as the door closed behind Coggins.

He pulled a letter opener from his desk drawer to pry the wax seal off the folded paper. "I hope so."

So busy had the Branstokes been with their new property, they had not had an opportunity to meet many other families in their vicinity, save for the vicar, Septimus Jones, and his wife, a woman of indeterminate age who delighted in gossip. When the vicar and his wife came for tea shortly after they'd arrived in the neighborhood, Mrs. Jones whispered to Lady Branstoke about the sad situation with Lord and Lady Aldrich at Bartlett Hall, their nearest neighboring estate.

"Baron Aldrich married a woman from trade," she disclosed. Mrs. Jones smoothed the fine blue cambric fabric of her skirts and admitted the Aldriches appeared content with their match, leastwise from what she saw at Sunday services. "However," she continued, "Lord Aldrich went away three weeks ago, hasn't returned, nor has anyone heard from him!"

Lamentably, the vicar's wife confided, the other prominent family, the Inglewoods of Inglewood Grange, looked down their noses at Lady Aldrich as she was not *to the manor born*.

"Now, Miranda," warned the vicar severely when he realized his wife was indulging in gossip.

"Well, Septimus, you know they are acting quite odious," she'd said primly, "even after you cautioned them against that unchristian attitude. They have continued to snub the Aldriches."

Cecilia's late husband had been in trade; consequently she knew how badly the *ton* treated a person coming from that economic stratus. Though she was born the granddaughter of a duke and the daughter of a baron, as the wife of a merchant, she was no one. Then when he died, miraculously she became a someone again in the eyes of the *ton*.

Cecilia could not bear that hypocrisy, and her heart bled for anyone else who might find themselves in a similar "neither fish nor fowl" situation. Upon the vicar's and his wife's departure, she immediately determined to make Lady Aldrich's acquaintance. And she was glad she had! The women became fast friends, visiting back and forth daily. Cecilia took it as her personal challenge to keep Lady Aldrich's spirits up during the continued absence of her husband, and she'd harried James to make discreet inquiries as to his location and the reason for his continued absence.

James had some acquaintance with the missing baron and knew him to be a bit of a loose screw and therefore did not see the need for the inquires his wife requested; however, newly married as they were, he indulged his beautiful wife and set the wheels in motion to learn more for her peace of mind.

He scanned the letter's contents, a frown pulling his dark brows together. He sighed deeply as he shook his head. He had to admit, his wife had excellent instincts. "A nasty business all around," he murmured.

"What is it, James?"

"It's from George Pollock, the magistrate in the Folkestone area. He said up the coast, between Folkestone and Dover, a carriage tumbled over a cliff. He believes the coach belonged to Lord Aldrich."

"What?!" She dropped her quill on the paper before her, ink blots splattering across the desk and her careful notes. She quickly grabbed another piece of paper to blot up wet ink.

James looked up from the letter. "Didn't you tell me Aldrich left on horseback?"

"That is what Elinor said," she responded as she frowned down at the ink mess. "It was just the coach?" she asked distractedly, as she searched for something else to clean the ink up with. She was loath to use her lace-edged handkerchief.

Seeing her dilemma, James handed her his handkerchief, then looked down at the paper again. "This is interesting. Pollock tells me they found no bodies at the location, yet he says he assumes Lord Aldrich is dead. He is, however, investigating further, but says that is not general knowledge. He has written directly to Lady Aldrich to inform her Lord Aldrich is dead!"

"Dead!" The color drained from Cecilia's face. "Oh no, poor Elinor!" She reached out, silently requesting to read the letter. James passed it to her.

Cecilia skimmed the missive, her expression stricken when she looked up at her husband again. "This is disastrous. Elinor has no one, James. Her mother is deceased, and her father is presently away on business in Scotland. She will be quite shattered. What a way to deliver the news, so matter-of-factly, so callously," she said.

"Magistrates must deal in facts, Cecilia," her husband reminded her, though he wondered how Mr. Pollock assumed death without proof.

"I know," she conceded petulantly, "but there is not a whit of sympathy or regret in this letter. I hope what he sent to Elinor had some bit of softness or regret. I must go see her immediately, James," she said, rising to her feet. She turned to quit the room.

James forestalled her with a light touch. "We'll go

together, my love," he said. There was much *not* stated in Mr. Pollock's letter and that fact troubled him, and knowing his wife, he knew she would soon tumble to that observation as well and would want to look for answers.

He crossed to the bell pull to ring for Coggins.

IN JUST OVER TWENTY MINUTES, James was driving them to Bartlett Hall.

Cecilia had harried their staff to hurry. She had sent Coggins to order a groom to harness the curricle with Sir James' grays and bring it around to the manor's front. She had sent the downstairs maid, previously employed in dusting the hall, to find Sarah, her maid, and send her to her while she ran up the stairs to her dressing room.

Minutes later, Sarah found her blindly yanking on the ribbons at the back of the peach and cream striped morning gown she'd donned before she'd gone down to breakfast.

"Here, your ladyship, leave off doing that lest you have it in knots," Sarah remonstrated.

"I'm in a hurry," Cecilia returned, pulling on the ribbon again.

Sarah pushed her hands out of the way and untangled the mess Cecilia had made. "Now, what has you in such a bother?"

"We have just had word that Lord Aldrich might be dead! We are going immediately to Bartlett Hall."

"Dead, you say?" Sarah questioned as she pulled the dress over Cecilia's head. "Did you know you have ink spots on this dress?"

"Yes, and yes," Cecilia said impatiently. "Please

fetch me the blue dress with the lace at the collar and cuffs."

Sarah laid the ruined morning gown across a chair by the window, then crossed to the armoire to pull out the blue gown. "This is a lovely dress, my lady. It goes beautifully with your eyes."

"Bother about me! Lady Aldrich is bound to be overwrought. I'm hoping it is a calming hue," Cecilia said.

"Definitely. Turn around, please, my lady, so that I can get these tapes."

"I'll want my kid half-boots, a vial of lavender water, and some extra handkerchiefs," Cecilia decided.

"Immediately," Sarah replied.

"I worry for Elinor," Cecilia told her husband as he tooled his matched grays down the drive toward Bartlett Hall.

"She has seemed a very level-headed young woman in the few times I have spoken with her," he said absently as he concentrated on his horses. He frowned at them. They hadn't been driven in a while and were restive. He must remind Romley to exercise them in harness and without.

"Oh, she is," his wife said, pulling him out of contemplation on his horses. "Which is why I believe we get on so marvelously. Though hers was an arranged marriage of convenience, she has fallen in love with her husband. This will devastate her, as it would me if I lost you," she said on a drawn-out sigh.

James glanced down at her and shifted the reins into one hand to reach over to squeeze her hands where they lay in her lap.

He privately acknowledged the same sentiment as he remembered his emotions when he'd realized she'd been abducted. That was five weeks ago. Sometimes when he awoke in the night with his heart racing, it seemed like yesterday.

The distance between Summerworth Park and Bartlett Hall was slightly more than a mile if one walked across the fields; however, by carriage it exceeded two miles along a pleasant lane with a vista of the rolling downs to the east. Wildflowers bloomed along the road and across the meadows.

"I will be interested to see the letter Mr. Pollock sent Lady Aldrich. I wonder if it contains more information than mine did," James said some minutes later as they turned down a tree-lined lane that would bring them to Bartlett Hall.

Cecilia looked up at him. "What more information should the letter have contained?"

"It's curious that he mentioned only the carriage as being at the bottom of the cliff. I doubt Aldrich drove a carriage without a horse or groom," he said.

"Oh!" Cecilia considered this observation. She frowned. "Could they all have been carried out to sea?"

"The people yes, I suppose; however, a horse or horses in harness would have stayed with the carriage."

Cecilia cocked her head. "That's true, and yet Mr. Pollock's letter gives no details. I wonder what kind of carriage it was?"

"Ha! Excellent point. I had been assuming a traveling carriage; however, it could have been a smaller vehicle, like a tilbury."

"And in that instance, there may not be a body for

it would have tumbled out of the equipage and therefore been washed out to sea."

"Yes, but that still leaves the question of the horse. And that is why I am curious if Lady Aldrich will show us her letter," James said.

"She will," Cecilia said. "I'll insist," she added, her brows pulling together in a frown.

Sir James, remembering how they met and Cecilia's fierce determination to find answers to her late husband's death, looked at his bride and smiled.

UNLIKE SUMMERWORTH PARK, Bartlett Hall revealed none of the deprivations a house might otherwise show from an impecunious owner. It was a neat nine-bay manor house built of Flemish yellow brick edged and banded with Kentish blue-gray ragstone. Deep green ivy climbed one corner of the building and framed an upper-story window. The roof was of dark gray slate.

As James swung the carriage around the drive before the house, Cecilia was surprised that neither a footman, groom, nor a stable lad ran up to greet them and to take their carriage. Cecilia could hear Elinor crying through the open library windows to the right of the centrally placed door. She tightly gripped her reticule with its vial of lavender water and extra handkerchiefs, glad she had thought to bring the items.

James handed Cecilia down from the carriage. "Are you sure you are ready for this?" he asked.

"Yes," she said decisively as she gathered her mantle of determination about her. "Take the carriage round to the stable yard. And then join me in the house."

"As you wish," he said, slight doubt coloring his voice as he looked up at the open window.

Cecilia hugged his arm, then pushed him on his way as she turned to walk toward the manor.

She sharply rapped the door knocker. When no one immediately answered, she tried the door latch. It was not locked, so she pushed the door open. She stood for a moment in the hallway, her eyes readjusting to the dimmer light inside after the bright light outdoors.

How odd. There were no servants immediately around.

Besides Elinor's sobbing, she now heard from the library a man's voice. Had Mr. Pollock come in person after all to give her the news of her husband's death? She walked toward the library's double doors. To her surprise, Cecilia heard the man asking Elinor about her husband's papers. Cecilia did not know what the stranger could want, but she deemed pestering a woman who had just learned she had lost her husband highly irregular and grossly rude. Curious and annoyed, she pushed open the library door.

Lady Aldrich sat on a green and cream damask-covered sofa near the fireplace. Her body turned away from the gentleman standing before her, her dark hair in disarray, her face buried in her arms. It was clear she was crying. That fact ratcheted up Cecilia's dissatisfaction with the man.

The gentleman was well-favored in appearance, tall, and most likely athletic, judging by how he held himself. When he turned in her direction, Cecilia noted his well-made clothing and the gloss on his boots. He was not a *tulip of the ton*, nor was he a dandy; however, he was neither a lawyer nor a clerk. She scowled.

"This is a private matter," the man said, his fair brows pulling together.

She looked him up and down. "Yes," Cecilia said in her haughtiest manner. She understood the power of the cut direct expression and used it on the gentleman. She was pleased to see him discomforted. "The death of Lord Aldrich is a private matter," she continued in a softer tone. "I suggest you leave."

She brushed past him and sat next to Elinor, pulling her around to cry on her shoulder. "I know, I know," she said soothingly while rubbing Elinor's back. "James and I are here for you."

Elinor lifted her head slightly to look at Cecilia. "How—" she hiccupped. "How did you know?"

"James has been making inquiries," she whispered as she pulled a fresh handkerchief from her reticule and blotted Elinor's cheeks. This started Elinor crying harder. Cecilia took her sodden handkerchief from her and put the fresh one in her hand.

"Madame! I do not know who you are, but it is of national importance that I speak with Lady Aldrich in private; she may have information that is vital for the government!" the man said, recovering from her initial presence. He took a step closer, flailing his arms for emphasis.

Cecilia glared up at him. "Nor do I know who you are!" Anger vibrated in her voice and posture. "I do know Lady Aldrich," she continued, "and I also know that what she doesn't need right now is a buffoon asking questions at her highest moment of grief! You are a caper-witted idiot to come here now, of all times and make demands! Get out!"

"Cecilia, is there a problem?" James calmly asked from the doorway, his demeanor not revealing any of the rancor he felt, first toward the servants he encountered in the servants' hall and now toward the puffed-up imbecile haranguing his wife and Lady Aldrich.

"Yes!" Cecilia replied. "This—this *nodcock* insists he speak with Elinor. When I came in, he was positively hounding her about some papers he thinks Lord Aldrich has. You can see she is in no condition to answer his questions, let alone think clearly if she could. Please get him out of here."

Twin red flags of color flared on Cecilia's cheeks, and her blue eyes turned their darkest blue, as they were wont to do when she was upset.

James studied the well-setup gentleman before him with patent disapproval. Military, he supposed. "Let's leave my wife to support and calm Lady Aldrich as best she can," he told the man in the voice he'd once used on his junior officers. He stepped aside to pointedly indicate the gentleman should proceed him out the door.

The man took a step forward, then stopped. "Who are you? You might be here for the same purpose as me," he protested, his broad brow furrowing, his lower lip thrust forward in the manner of a child's pout.

James sighed. "I have no idea what your purpose is. I am Sir James Branstoke, and the fair-haired woman you have riled is my wife, Lady Branstoke, granddaughter of the Duke of Houghton. Now come, Lieutenant."

"Captain," corrected the gentleman stiffly, raising his chin to look down his aquiline nose at Branstoke.

His manner amused James. "My apologies, *Captain*," he said. "Now I insist we leave the women in peace. We can adjourn to the blue parlor I know to be across the hall here and see if we can rouse the staff from their mourning to offer us refreshments."

The captain frowned, but this time did as James

requested. James quietly shut the library door after them. The captain turned to look at him.

"How did you know?" he asked.

"Know what?" James said as they crossed the broad entry hall. "That you are military?"

"Yes."

"Your stance," he returned simply.

"Damn and blast it," the man said viciously.

James smiled, his eyes hooded. "I take it you are trying to conceal your military association?" James asked as he pushed open the parlor doors.

"It is not in the best interest of the mission for me to be identified as a member of the military."

"And why is that?" James asked languidly as he went to the bell pull to summon a servant to them.

"That, sir, is confidential," the man answered stiffly.

James studied the man. He had a firm chin and dimples in his cheeks even when he didn't smile. He reminded James of someone.

"And is knowing your name confidential as well?" he asked as he sat in a chair by the window, his face in shadows while the guest stood in bright light. "I warn you, if you say your name is confidential, then I should say you are the villain here and will notify authorities that you have been behaving suspiciously to Lady Aldrich."

The man compressed his lips in a tight line. "Melville, Captain Andrew Melville."

"Ah," James said, the dimples and chin coalescing into another face in his mind. "Any relationship to Lady Blessingame?"

"She is my sister," he reluctantly replied.

"She is an intelligent woman and from what I understand, she has served the crown well."

The door to the parlor opened. "Mr. Thomas," James said, "if you would be so kind, some brandy for us, and then please see that your mistress and my wife receive refreshments in the library as well."

Earlier, when James had driven the curricle around to the stable, he'd been irritated at the absence of staff. He'd tied his horses off at the gate and come in the house by the back servants' entry, where he found all the staff gathered in the servants' hall crying, commiserating, or wringing their hands, wondering what was to become of them.

James had introduced himself and sternly reminded them of their obligation to their mistress. It was she who would determine what would happen to them, and it was she they should care for. They quickly scattered save for the butler, who quietly introduced himself as Roland Thomas. He apologized for himself and the staff and thanked James for his arrival and his reminder.

Now that worthy merely bowed and murmured acquiescence. He went to a cabinet that sat under a large landscape painting of an old oak tree with a mill in the background. From inside, he pulled out a decanter with two glasses, placed them on a small silver tray on top of the cabinet, then brought them over to where James sat. He then bowed himself out of the room.

James poured out two glasses of brandy, handed one to Melville, and then gestured for Captain Melville to sit as he asked, "Did you bring Lady Aldrich the news of the probable death of Baron Aldrich?"

Captain Melville moved toward the chair nearest James. "No, though it appeared she had recently learned that news, news that is distressing to me as well." He started to sit, then straightened and looked at James. "What do you mean by probable death?"

James lifted a shoulder in an elegant shrug. "It is my understanding there is no body or bodies." He sniffed the brandy. The rich aroma suggested smuggled goods. His sip confirmed his suspicion. He smiled slightly as he set the glass on the gilt bronze and ormolu decorated table at his side. "But if you were not aware of his death," he continued, "then why are you here when Lord Aldrich is away? What do you want of Lady Aldrich?"

"That I cannot tell you; I can only say it is of national importance," Melville said lugubriously.

"If you won't say, then I cannot help you," James said. "And I very much doubt Lady Aldrich can either."

The captain ran his hand through his dusky blond hair. "If I could but look through his desk," he said plaintively.

James raised one dark brow in haughty disdain. "No, that is not possible. For one, I expect Lady Aldrich and my wife to be in there for some time; for another," he spread his hands before him, "I don't trust you."

Melville gaped at James. "But, but..."

"You have displayed a marked want of good manners. Your methods are crude and not at all good ton. I believe it would mortify your sister. I suggest you finish your drink, for you are leaving now," James said calmly.

The captain bristled and looked like he wanted to protest further; however, under the circumstances, there was nothing more he could say. He rose from his chair and looked blackly at James as he stalked out of the room and took his hat from a waiting footman.

James watched him go, his eyes narrowed as he considered the man and what his errand could be. That he was Lady Blessingame's brother, and was reticent in manner, inclined James to think the young man worked clandestinely, as had Lady Blessingame's late husband, and at one time, Lady Blessingame herself. Interesting. What could he want from Aldrich? The baron was a likeable enough fellow, his intellect not above average. Though he did not know him well, he understood someone always talked him into schemes and games his peers entered into, thus his need this year to take a wife with funds.

He tossed off the rest of his brandy, stood up, turning to the window. He saw a stable lad bring a horse around for the captain and he watched the man ride down the lane he and Cecilia had arrived on. When he was out of sight, James walked out of the room and crossed the hall, back to the library.

He doubted they had seen the last of Captain Melville.

2

Outside the library hovered the butler and two women, one of whom Branstoke judged to be the housekeeper by her dark, somber attire and chatelaine, and the other, an East Indian woman draped in a cream-colored saree banded in dark brown and yellow.

He cleared his throat. "Excuse me," he said.

"Oh!" the housekeeper exclaimed as they all stepped back from eavesdropping.

"Mrs. Wembly, have a bedchamber made up for Lady Branstoke and me. Under the circumstances, we will stay here the night. I'll write a note that one of the grooms can take to Summerworth Park to apprise them and arrange for my valet and her lady's maid to join us."

"Yes, Sir James," the woman bobbed a curtsy.

"Lady Branstoke and I will endeavor to see that Lady Aldrich retires to her chambers. She is understandably overwrought. I trust you have some laudanum to help her sleep?"

It was the tiny Indian woman who answered. "Yes, sahib. I go up, fix memsahib's room and get medicine," she said in a heavily accented, singsong voice, her dark brown eyes liquid with unshed tears as she looked up at him.

"Excellent." He opened the library door and went inside.

Lady Aldrich reclined on the sofa, her feet drawn up and covered with a burnt orange shawl, the fringe brushing the floor. She no longer cried, though her face bore the imprint of her tears, her skin pale and blotchy. She clutched a handkerchief in her hand.

Cecilia had pulled up an upholstered chair next to Lady Aldrich, her expression the saddest Sir James could ever recall seeing on his wife. She looked up at him.

James gave her a consoling nod. "I have gotten rid of the gentleman plaguing Lady Aldrich. However, I don't have confidence that he will stay away for long. I have therefore taken the liberty of telling the staff to ready rooms for us." With a look at Lady Aldrich, he added, "I trust, my lady, that I did not overstep my bounds?"

Lady Aldrich reached out pale fingers to him. "No, no. Thank you," she whispered.

He took her hand in his and bowed over it. "We are your friends and neighbors, Lady Aldrich, we could do no less."

"Oh, please call me Elinor, as Cecilia does. I should be much more comfortable if you do."

He squeezed her fingers and smiled at her. "I should be delighted to, my lady, and by the same token you must call me James." He straightened. " Now, do you think you could stand? We will help you to your room. Your maid has gone to prepare it for you and fetch a small dose of laudanum to help you sleep. When you awaken, we can plan what we need to do next."

"You are too kind," she said with a tentative, wan smile as she struggled to sit up straighter.

With Cecilia's assistance, James helped the young woman to her feet and guided her across the room. With each step she seemed to pull on strength from inside and walked a little straighter, a little firmer. By the time they reached the door, she stood unsupported.

"Very good, Elinor," Sir James murmured, pleased to see the way she pulled herself together. She was not a vaporish female. She would get through this personal disaster better than most women. Quite like Cecilia.

At the stairs she thanked Mr. Thomas and Mrs. Wembly for their attention and apologized for her collapse that afternoon.

"Oh, no, my lady!" exclaimed Mrs. Wembly as she hurried to her mistress's side. "It is not to be wondered. Please, don't fratch yourself. Now, let me help you upstairs, my lady."

"Thank you. Oh, one thing." Elinor turned to look back at her butler. "Please follow whatever instructions Sir James or Lady Branstoke give you. I am not in a condition to think clearly right now."

"Of course, my lady," said Mr. Thomas.

Cecilia slipped her arm through Sir James' arm and leaned her head against his shoulder as they watched her climb the stairs with Mrs. Wembly. Once the pair had safely made the landing, James guided his wife back toward the library.

"We have much to discuss, my dear."

"Yes! Tell me about that gentleman who was here. He seemed quite insistent that Elinor knew something or had something he urgently needed. I asked her if she knew what he wanted. She vehemently said she didn't, which set off another bout of tears."

"His name is Andrew Melville. Captain Andrew Melville."

"Ah, that explains it. He did not have the manner of a clerk or lawyer or banker, I was thinking. Though his clothing was rather nondescript, his jacket was well-tailored, and his boots gleamed."

James laughed. "Yes, I believe Captain Melville thought himself to be in disguise," he drawled.

His wife harrumphed. "Hardly. If he is with the foreign office, it is no wonder Britain has struggled so against Boney. A little young for a captain, isn't he?" She sat down in a chair by the desk.

"When I mentioned Lady Blessingame's name for the likeness I saw in him to her, he admitted to a sibling relationship. That means he's a younger son of Thomas Melville, the Earl of Cuberton. I'm sure the earl arranged Melville's commission—and arranged for his assignment to the foreign office as well." He took a seat on the other side of the desk.

"I've heard you mention Lady Blessingame before. I have never met the woman."

"You would like her. She wasn't in London for the season this year. She's been staying with her sister. I shall definitely have to introduce you and you will see the resemblance to Captain Melville."

It surprised Cecilia to feel a small spurt of jealousy at how warmly James spoke of the woman.

"Have you seen the letter Elinor received from Pollock?" James asked, shaking her out of her thoughts.

"The missive that put her into this sad state? Why no! I wonder where it is," she mused.

She leaped to her feet, spinning round to look about the room. "It is bound to be in here somewhere." She looked about, then walked to where a shaft of early afternoon sun illuminated the jewel-tones of the beautiful Axminster carpet. By the window, she stooped to pick up a folded paper.

"Well done, my dear!" Branstoke said.

She laughed as she handed the letter to him. "It occurred to me that this room is quite dim and if I were to read a letter in here without recourse to having candles lit, I would stand by a window."

"Very good, my love!" He unfolded the letter. "It is from Mr. Pollock," he said as he, too, turned to the light to read. "It says much the same as mine. But he says Baron Aldrich's portmanteau was still strapped to the back. That is how he concluded Lord Aldrich is dead."

"That hardly seems conclusive," Cecilia said.

"I agree." He looked up, staring across the room as he tapped the letter's folded edge against his opposite hand.

"What is it, James?"

He shook his head. "Too many questions swirling in my brain, my dear." He ran his hand through his hair, then pushed the letter across the table toward her. "Here, you read it," he said.

"Thank you." She picked it up and quickly read. Sadly, she agreed, it didn't offer more insight than they had already gleaned from his letter to Sir James. "Just by his frustrating letters, I find I already dislike Mr. Pollock," she said.

Her husband laughed.

"Well, then, we'd best get on discovering some answers ourselves." She crossed to the bellpull. "You said you had letters to write. I should send messages to Sarah and Mrs. Vernon."

"Mr. Thomas," she said when he opened the door.

"Where might we find pen, paper, and ink?"

The butler crossed the room to the desk. "Here you are, my lady," he said as he opened the drawer and pulled out the requested items.

"Excellent. Can you please have some candles lit in here so we might write some letters? And I'd like tea with a light repast served here as well."

"Of course." He proceeded to light the candelabra on the mantel, which he then carried over to the desk. Then he crossed to a cabinet against the windows and pulled out a cut crystal decanter of port, along with a glass, and set them on top of the cabinet.

"Thank you, Mr. Thomas," Cecilia said with a smile.

James looked up. "Mr. Thomas, would you answer a question?"

"Certainly, sir, if I can."

"How long has Lady Aldrich had an East Indian maid?"

"I can't say, sir, she came with her when she married Lord Aldrich. She's a quiet little thing and devoted to Lady Aldrich."

"Hmm. Thank you."

Mr. Thomas bowed again and left the room.

"Elinor has an ayah?" Cecilia asked.

"So it would appear."

"I did not know that. All the time I've been here, Elinor has not mentioned her, nor have I seen her. I wonder if she was one of those unfortunates who traveled to England with a family returning from India and upon arrival here was let go?"

"Possibly. People who bring ayahs with them to care for their children on the journey are supposed to provide the passage back to India, but many don't."

"I know. I have read some sad stories. I shall have

to ask Elinor," Cecilia said. She pulled a sheet of paper before her and unstoppered the ink. "Now, James, who are you going to write to?"

"Besides sending a return note to Mr. Pollock, I should write to our Summerworth Park staff. And I think I shall send a note to Mr. Thornbridge to see what he can discover about our Captain Melville."

"An excellent idea! David has a talent for investigation."

"He appears to. After the sale of Waddley Spice and Tea, perhaps we should see to setting him up in the inquiry business.

Cecilia clasped her hands together delightedly and nearly bounced off her chair in her enthusiasm for that idea. "What an excellent plan!" Then she frowned. "But only so long as he promises to stay away from the docks," she said, remembering the unfortunate occurrence during his last investigation on a dock.

Sir James laughed.

THE NEXT MORNING, the Branstokes were surprised and delighted to see Lady Aldrich enter the breakfast parlor. She was dressed in a plain, dove gray gown and wore her hair pulled back into a tight bun. She looked more like a governess than a wife mourning her husband.

James rose from his chair.

She paused in the doorway. "I don't have any proper mourning attire. My maid, Aisha, is altering a dress of Mrs. Wembley's for me until I can order my widow's clothing. This is the best I could do this morning," she apologized, her voice small and hesitant, her brown eyes in her pale, wan face imploring their understanding.

Cecilia's heart went out to her. "Gracious, Elinor, dear friend! Please don't worry about your mourning wardrobe," she exclaimed.

"How are you feeling this morning?" Sir James asked. He pulled out a chair for her at the head of the table before the footman could do so. He signaled for the waiting man to prepare a plate for Lady Aldrich.

"I'm much better, thank you. The first shock has worn off. I don't know why, but I feel numb now. Disembodied, somehow," she said pensively. Then she shook herself and gave a little laugh. "I am being silly."

"No, not at all," Sir James gently assured her.

Cecilia smiled softly. "This is all so sudden," she said. "Give yourself time."

She sighed. "I know, and I will," she said earnestly. "I do confess I have not written to my father in the last five weeks to apprise him of Simon's absence. I should have. Now, I wish my father weren't so far away in Scotland for the sheep sales," she said as the footman placed a plate in front of her. She looked up and murmured her thanks.

"Your father trades in sheep?" Sir James asked.

"Not quite. He trades in sheep's *wool*. The Scottish sheep have a much finer wool than some of our English sheep," she explained. "While much raw English and Scottish wool is sent to mills overseas, he has several small wool cloth manufactories in England. He thinks it a travesty that our wool goes out of the country for spinning, and then we are made to pay import taxes to get it back as cloth," she said as she took a bite of food. It tasted surprisingly good. She hadn't thought she would be hungry and was pleasantly astonished to discover she was.

"I should like to meet your father sometime," James said. "Perhaps he can advise me on the best sheep to have at Summerworth Park. Being on the edge of the Downs, this is too fine an area not to take advantage of sheep pasturing."

"Yes, Simon and I have been— Oh," her voice dropped to a whisper. "I mean, we *had* been discussing sheep for Bartlett Hall." She hung her head down, squeezing her eyes tight. "I told myself I would not cry anymore," she said, her voice shaking.

"It is okay to cry," Cecilia assured her. She rose from her chair at the table and crossed to the sideboard. She poured tea into a cup and took it to Elinor. "Here, there is something rather bracing about morning tea, I think. It will help."

Elinor accepted the teacup with a slight smile. "Thank you." She turned in her chair to look at them both. "And thank you for coming to my rescue yesterday. That was so strange," she said pensively, "how that man kept insisting Simon had papers he needed. I do not know what he meant. Simon is not one for paperwork of any kind."

Sir James smiled slightly. Knowing Baron Simon Aldrich as he did through his clubs in London, he could well believe Lord Aldrich had a dislike of paperwork. Aldrich was a likeable-enough fellow; however, his competence was not large, and he appeared to live beyond his means. Society rumors said he married for money.

"Elinor, much as I am loath to bring it up, have you thought of contacting Lord Aldrich's family, and his solicitor? And what about his estate steward? They all need to be notified of his passing."

Elinor blinked rapidly, then sat up straighter, placing her hands together in her lap. "I am not convinced Simon is dead," she said carefully. She looked at them a little fearfully, steeling herself against protest.

The Branstokes stared quizzically at her.

She nodded, encouraged by their expressions. "I do not feel it here," she said, laying a hand on her heart. "So, I do not wish to be too precipitous until I am certain."

"But, my dear lady—" James began.

She held her palm up to halt his words. "I have decided I must see where this Pollock gentleman claims Simon died. I intend to leave this afternoon." She raised her chin defiantly, then lowered it slightly when neither of the Branstokes immediately protested.

James inclined his head to her, then leaned back in his chair. He took a sip of coffee. "I understand. I, too, have questions. It is my intention to go to the coast to investigate. I can go as your surrogate."

Elinor took in a large breath, then expelled it quickly. She compressed her lips a moment before saying, "I very much appreciate that, sir, but I still wish to go as well. I need to see the scene with my eyes, not through another's eyes," she said primly.

The Branstokes exchanged glances.

"You know, James, I would say much the same," Cecilia said. She laid her hand on Elinor's shoulder as she looked down at her. "Well, we shall all go."

"Cecilia!" protested her husband.

"No, James. I understand her feelings and concerns." She sat down again. "I think we should support her in this."

James stared at his wife for a moment, then slowly nodded. A slight smile lit his eyes as he looked up at his wife. Sunlight through the breakfast-room window lit her pale blond hair around her head like an angel's halo. Where was the vaporous, flighty woman of less than six weeks ago?

"All right. I shall plan," he said. "But I would prefer we put off leaving until tomorrow."

"But—" began Elinor.

"Hear me out, please. I sent off some inquiries yesterday. I would like to see if I receive any responses. Furthermore, I believe the accident location is a good half day's drive away, but we need to know from Mr. Pollock exactly where it is before we go haring off. In addition, we shall have to stay in the area as a drive there and back in one day will be too hard on the horses. I shall send ahead for rooms. We will need two carriages, one for us to travel in and one for our servants and luggage."

"I think traveling with a retinue would slow us down," Cecilia said briskly. "I can pack light, and I do not need Sarah to dress and undress me. What do you think, Elinor, can we ladies maid each other?" she asked brightly.

The tightness in Elinor's shoulders released and she visibly relaxed with a long exhale. "Yes, yes, I imagine we could," she said earnestly. She smiled then, and her face lit up.

"Good, it will be an adventure," Cecilia said, gratified to see the color coming back into Elinor's cheeks. "Then, that is settled. We leave early tomorrow."

James dabbed his lips with his napkin and rose from his place at the table. "Then, if you ladies will excuse me, I should begin preparations for our journey."

3

Cecilia could have wished for a brighter, sunnier day for the journey. The heavy gray clouds with their darker bottoms threatened to release torrents of rain. A perpetual wind whipped the tree branches. She worried for James, who rode on horseback alongside the carriage. He would be drenched should the clouds' seams rip apart.

Her maid, Sarah, had argued fiercely against Cecilia traveling without her. Sarah was fiercely protective of her employer, given the events in London a few weeks past when she was kidnapped. Cecilia did not let the past rule her lest she be pulled back into doldrums, for there was much in her past she would sooner forget. However, the events of the past brought her together with Sir James Branstoke and so she could not dwell on the bad for the blessing she had received in the person of her new husband.

The carriage rocked and bounced as they turned off the more well-traveled road to a local road, rougher than the main road from Maidstone to Folkestone. Elinor stirred. Cecilia watched her as she blinked her eyes a few times while coming out of her drowsed state.

"Where are we?" she asked.

"I don't precisely know," Cecilia said. "However, we are no longer on the main road, so I surmise we are nearing the cliffs and the site of the incident."

Lady Elinor Aldrich looked out the carriage windows. "Have we passed the ruined church yet?"

"Yes, probably ten minutes ago."

"I'm sorry to have missed it. Simon brought me to it for a picnic once. I quite love that ruin. It's called St. Phineas the Protector." She turned to look at Cecilia. "I feel there is a ghostly romance to that old church. Simon and I agreed that if we were to ever build a folly on the estate, we would prefer a replica of that church to one of those miniature Greek temple follies that are popular. Rather a whimsical notion, I know," Elinor said with a smile and a faraway look in her eyes.

"I think that is a delightful idea! Now you have me curious about the ruin. I will have to visit it with James one day."

"Take a picnic lunch with you." She glanced out the window again. "But make sure it is a sunny day."

Cecilia laughed. "Assuredly."

"I've never traveled past the church. It looks quite barren and windswept here, does it not?" Elinor mused.

"Yes, that it does."

"It does not strike me as a place my husband would visit. He is a social man. While I love the wide-open space and solitude, Simon prefers his towns and cities where he might meet convivial acquaintances."

Cecilia listened, but could find nothing to say as she had never met Lord Aldrich.

"Ours was an arranged marriage," Elinor said, staring down at her clasped hands in her lap.

"I know," Cecilia answered softly.

"You do?" She looked up at her in surprise. "—Oh, of course you do. Society talks," she said with a heavy sigh. "Simon laughingly says he has no head for money, nor for economy." She smiled. "He is not a bad man, just no one thought to teach him. In those fancy schools he went to, they taught about long-dead philosophers and some of the scientific world, I think. But not about practical matters."

Cecilia questioned if he had not been taught, or if it was more likely that he hadn't paid attention.

Elinor laughed as she stared blindly ahead, a smile on her lips, her thoughts far away. "He is determined to prove to me he can be more that a London dandy. So silly." She frowned. "That is why he took this trip. One last thing he said he had to do before he could settle down with me in wedded bliss. And those were his exact words. He had me laughing."

Her voice broke on her last words. Tears rolled down her cheeks again. She quickly dabbed at her cheeks with a lace-edged handkerchief. "I'm so sorry. I was determined to put tears behind me."

"Please," Cecilia implored. "No apologies. As I have said before, you have every right to your sorrow and tears."

The carriage hit a deep rut and threw Elinor into Cecilia, knocking her bonnet askew, the feathers tickling Cecilia's nose.

"Oh! Oh!" *Achoo!* She held a gloved hand up against her nose to thwart another sneeze—to no avail. *Achoo! Achoo!*

Elinor quickly straightened as Cecilia fumbled for her handkerchief.

Cecilia looked at Elinor, her eyes watering from the sneezes, her nose pink. Together, the women started to laugh.

"Before I met Sir James, I feigned ill health so others would ignore me. But I could never feign a good sneeze," Cecilia said as she dabbed at the corners of her eyes and her nose with her embroidered handkerchief.

"Pretended sickness?" Elinor asked, her eyes wide.

"Yes, I pretended a vaporish constitution. It was amazing how society tolerated my presence to the extent I went unnoticed and people around me talked freely! The only person who didn't believe my illnesses was the calm, perpetually bored Sir James Branstoke," she declared with a laugh. "His curiosity is how we became acquainted."

The carriage rocked hard once more, then stopped. Cecilia looked out the window to see James ride up to the carriage and dismount. He approached the carriage door, opened it, and set the steps.

"We are here," he said somberly. He helped first Cecilia and then Elinor to step down from the carriage.

Though it was late spring, a chilly breeze blew up from the cliff edge. It was early afternoon; however, the uniform gray sky could have been at any time of day—morning, late afternoon—it would be the same. Nothing within view but the slightly rolling grassy headlands. Cecilia wished she had a muff. While she wore gloves, she felt she would feel warmer if her hands were warmer. The wind caught at her bonnet, she bent her head down against the onslaught.

"Are you certain you want to see the wreckage?" James asked Elinor.

"Yes, James. I am determined." Her eyes were clear, and her lips set in a straight line.

James smiled slightly, admiring her staunch manner.

"Well, then, let's get this over with. See the stake over there with the kerchief tied to it? I had my man ride ahead and mark the spot so it would be easy to find. He has also arranged accommodations in the village down the road," he told them.

He offered an arm to each woman, and they made their way to the stake at the cliff edge.

At this location, the drop to the English Channel below was not straight down. There were small plateaus. As they looked down, they could see the wreck of the carriage on one of those plateaus. Fierce, wind-driven waves slammed against the rocks below the wreckage, trying to claim it for the channel, but the carriage stopped too high for the waves to reach. It looked like it had rolled and bounced down a bit before settling on that ledge. It was, as James had originally assumed, a heavy traveling carriage. The fall heavily bashed the carriage frame. No one inside the carriage could have lived. The shaft was gone. It did not look as if horses had gone over with the carriage. Interesting, Sir James thought as he looked down.

"Can we get down there?" Elinor asked in a distant, flat voice.

Sir James and Cecilia looked at her.

"I should like to see if there is any blood in the carriage," she whispered, her eyes wide in her pinched face. James felt the tension radiating through her body from where her arm linked to his.

"Ah, I see how your thoughts are going. A man would need to rappel down, as I assume someone did, to recover your husband's portmanteau. I shall make inquiries as to what they observed about the wreck, and if need be, I shall rappel down to investigate."

"James!" protested Cecilia. The wind whipped her

bonnet ribbons. She caught at them with one of her gloved hands.

He looked down at her. "While climbing down is needful, it should not be dangerous so long as I do it in little to no wind. And I have more faith in my powers of observation than that of others."

She sighed. "True." She shivered as a new gust of wind blew across them. It forced her to take a slight step back. Her husband's arm through hers kept her from falling.

"Lady Aldrich—Elinor, have you seen enough for now?"

"Yes, yes, I have," Elinor said. "However, I should like to know more," she said resolutely.

"As would I," James assured her. "Now, let me get you both back to the carriage. It is cold out here; the wind is increasing, and I fear the horses are uneasy in this wind."

MINUTES LATER, the carriage drove under the brick archway leading to the courtyard of The Seagull Coaching Inn and Tavern. An old wattle and daub building across the courtyard spoke to the original age of the establishment. The stables in the newer front brick addition were larger than the original inn itself, which also saw additions made to it over the years with a wing of rooms to the left of the original building, accessible from exterior stairs and walkways. Men and boys ran in and out of the stables and into the inn with purpose. Cecilia laughed softly as the image of ants at an anthill flashed in her mind.

Their carriage had scarcely drawn up before the inn when the door was flung open, steps set, and a young man held out his hand to assist Cecilia and Elinor. The minute they were out of the carriage and John Coachman had descended the box, the young man scampered up in his place and drove the carriage toward the stable.

"That was fast," Elinor said, watching their coach drive away.

"And efficient. I just hope they remember to get our portmanteaus," Cecilia said.

"They will, Lady Branstoke," assured John Coachman gruffly.

"I had heard The Seagull is proud of their efficiency," James said, coming up beside them. "Now I can see why. Come, I would get you ladies inside and in front of a warm fire."

Cecilia looked around the open room they'd entered. She liked what she saw. Dark, old wood log beams ran across the ceiling, supported by other old wood logs. The walls were whitewashed above table-height wood paneling. Gas lamps hung from wrought iron hooks pounded into the columns. A fire blazed in the enormous fireplace that dominated one end of the room. A few people were seated in chairs near the fireplace, but it was early in the day, that time between the departures of last night's visitors and the arrivals of this night's visitors.

Just then, the innkeeper came out from a back room to greet them, a portly gentleman with a ruddy complexion and a broad smile that lit his face. "Welcome to The Seagull, Sir James! My name is Tinsley, Edward Tinsley. I received your note yesterday afternoon, and all is in readiness. My ladies, my daughter, Daphne, here," he said, waving his hand toward the comely young redhead that stood a little back, "will escort you upstairs so you might freshen up."

Daphne bobbed a curtsy.

"Sir James, if you don't mind, I'd like a word with you before you go up," the innkeeper said earnestly. He wrung his hands against his prominent belly.

"Of course," James said. He turned to Cecilia. "I shall be right up after I talk to Mr. Tinsley, here."

She nodded and followed Daphne toward an interior set of stairs.

"John Coachman, go on into the pub for a pint. Have them put it on my tab," James told his coachman.

The coachman nodded and tromped away toward the fireplace.

"After you," James told Mr. Tinsley.

"Sir James, I know from your man who came by yesterday that you are here to find out more about the carriage that went over the cliff. If you would follow me to the stables, I have something intriguing to show you," Mr. Tinsley said, leading him toward the large stable the ostler had driven their carriage into.

James followed the publican to a small stall toward the back. When Mr. Tinsley opened the gate, James saw inside a broken carriage shaft.

"The reason we discovered the accident 'twere 'acause of the horses dragging this carriage shaft and harness rigging about. They were nervous, but exhausted. I figured they tried to break free, but only ended up more tangled in the reins. My man had ta cut a couple of them reins. Horses were so entangled and too frightened to stand still for him to untangle them. 'Twere a mite cut up from thrashing about, too. I have them restin' in the pasture at one of the neighbor farms."

Sir James looked the man over. "You are a good

man, Mr. Tinsley. I see your reputation as a good and honest innkeeper is well deserved."

"Only way I know, sir. But the reason we went lookin' fer the carriage is 'acause of this," he said, pointing to the end of the broken shaft.

Branstoke looked down at the broken end, then quickly squatted down to get a better look.

"It's partially sawed through!"

"Aye, sir. That's why we sent fer the magistrate straightaway," Mr. Tinsley said, staring down at the broken shaft.

Branstoke ran his fingers over the wood. "It appears someone forcibly struck the non-sawed side to encourage the break. Did anyone go down to the carriage?"

"Aye, my man Jeremy. Couple of others held the rope to help him down and back up. He's the one who brought up the fellow's case."

"Were there no signs of any bodies about?" James asked.

"No, sar."

"What about blood in the carriage?"

Mr. Tinsley scratched his head. "We did not think on that, but there weren't none that Jeremy saw."

James rose to his feet. "And you say the magistrate has the portmanteau now?"

"Aye, sar, and he sent men down to investigate, too. They were swarming all over it. They almost lost one gent with their carelessness. All that climbing about the carriage made it shift again to the cliff edge," he said, shaking his head.

"How far away is this magistrate?" James asked, a frown pulling his brows together. Much as he disliked the idea, he thought he needed to see this magistrate as soon as possible.

"'Bout a two-hour ride to Denwidth Park, I'd say. That's his estate, jest the other side of Folkestone."

James let out a breath he hadn't known he'd been holding. "Do you have a fresh horse I might rent?" he asked grimly.

"Aye, that we do. But if you go today, don't be thinkin' to come back today," Mr. Tinsley warned.

"Why not? I could change horses before I return and pay for its return to you tomorrow."

"It ain't the horses that be the most concarn. To be honest, sar, lately, roads here aren't safe at night. Mr. Pollock and others been investigatin' the mischief, but don't have no solution yet. And 'asides, that Mr. Pollock, he be a talkative gent and he'll be interviewing you to see what you might know of this Lord Simon Aldrich fellow."

Branstoke crossed his arms over his chest as he thought about Mr. Tinsley's advice. His brow furrowed. He felt the pressure of time. This was best not left to another day; however, to journey to the magistrate would mean leaving Cecilia and Elinor here. He stared at the broken shaft a moment more. He looked up at Mr. Tinsley.

"I trust you and your people can safeguard Lady Branstoke and Lady Aldrich?"

"Of a certainty, Sar James. 'Twould be an honor."

JAMES OPENED the door to the room Daphne directed him to and found his wife reading in a chair near the window.

"Cecilia."

"Oh, there you are, James," she said, rising and crossing to him. She wrapped her arms around him.

He dropped a light kiss on her hair, then set her away from him. "We must talk."

"Why, what has happened?" she asked, looking up at his face. His habitual languid expression was replaced with concern writ large across his brow by the furrows she saw there.

"Mr. Tinsley wanted to show me the shaft from Aldrich's carriage."

"It's here?" she asked.

"Yes, one of his men found the horses still in harness to the shaft and brought them here. The horses are at a nearby farm; however, Mr. Tinsley has the shaft here. There is evidence that the carriage falling down the cliff was not an accident," he told her.

"How so?"

"The shaft was partially sawed through," he grimly explained.

"Aah!" Cecilia exclaimed, raising her hand to her mouth, her blue eyes wide open.

"Let's sit."

As he led her to an upholstered chair by the fireplace, sat down and pulled her into his lap, he looked about the room. "This is an unusually large room for an inn."

Cecilia laughed. "I thought so, too. I'm sure is has an unusually large tariff to match its large size."

Branstoke raised an eyebrow at that observation but didn't comment. "Tinsley sent a man down the cliff to the carriage. He says he found no signs of bodies, nor of blood within the carriage, and it had tumbled quite a bit."

"So, Simon could be alive."

"I would not wish to get Elinor's hopes up, but yes. That is why I am riding out this afternoon to visit the magistrate and retrieve Lord Aldrich's portmanteau, and hopefully get some answers as to what the magistrate might have discovered."

"That sounds like a wise plan," Cecilia said, laying her head on his shoulder.

"The downside to this plan is I will need to stay the night near the magistrate. I understand he is on the other side of Folkestone."

Cecilia raised her head. "Why?" she asked. Her lips tightened into a thin line. "Is he that far away? Shouldn't you perhaps wait until the morrow and all of us go?"

"I have an itch at the back of my neck that tells me I should go now. I suggest, now that I see the size of this room, that you and Elinor stay in this room. Tinsley has vowed to watch over you."

Cecilia didn't look happy; however, she sighed and agreed. "It will help us act as maid to each other. I truthfully hadn't thought that through before I made the suggestion. Rather difficult being in different rooms. Staying together would solve that problem."

He laughed lightly at that, then said, "Tomorrow, when I return, we shall travel back to Summerworth Park. I still have my other queries out."

"Agreed. Let me talk to Elinor, then." She smiled. "She can be a stubborn woman for all she is shy and retiring. I quite enjoy her company."

"Hopefully that stubborn streak will give her strength. This is a mystery that I hope has a good end."

"But you are not sure," Cecilia said, gazing up at him.

"No, I'm not," he admitted with a sigh.

4

"Comin in, come in, Sir James. I've been expecting you," said Mr. Pollock as he rose from behind his desk in the library.

The butler, who had admitted James to the house, was built like a prizefighter, thick neck, broad shouldered, large hands, beetle-browed. He looked like a Gentleman Jackson's employee, not a man to be butler to a magistrate.

The room he had shown him into was an opulent library filled with bronze statues, marble busts, large paintings depicting various sports, and enough books to keep the library appellation.

"Please, have a seat," Pollock said, indicating one of the two wing chairs covered in East Indian crewel embroidery fabric that were drawn up before the mammoth, carved stone fireplace. "Yesterday, when your man approached me, he indicated you would be traveling down here in the company of Lady Aldrich?" he said, gently probing.

Sir James nodded, inwardly smiling at the magistrate's seemingly gentle inquiry. "Lady Branstoke and I felt she should not be alone."

Mr. Pollock nodded as he leaned back in his chair

behind the desk. "Admirable, admirable," he acknowledged. "And where are the ladies now?"

"At The Seagull."

"Ah yes, the estimable establishment of Mr. Edward Tinsley." Pollock's voice relaxed into a friendly
mien. "I assume he showed you the carriage shaft?"

"Yes, he did. And he informed me you had men
investigate the wreckage?" James said, aping Pollocks
insouciance.

"I did. Unfortunately, other than the portmanteau
I mentioned in my letter to Lady Aldrich, there was
nothing else to find," Pollock said.

"No signs of bodies, or blood?"

Pollock shook his head. "No, none."

"So, what do you make of this carriage down a cliff,
sawed shaft, no bodies?"

Mr. Pollock waved his hand up in a dismissive gesture. "Staged, of course. Most likely smuggler quarrels.
I'd say Lord Aldrich is dead and the carriage over the
cliff is both a warning and an attempt to forestall any
search for the body. Smugglers are a vicious lot. I've
heard Lord Aldrich was purse pinched. Many a man
has attempted to recover money through smuggling,
mostly to a terrible end."

James considered the form of smuggling Cecilia's
former husband and brother had been in and thought
the magistrate did not know how correct he was. But
Aldrich a smuggler? Branstoke did not know the man
well; however, he'd venture smuggling would not be a
route Aldrich would choose, unless blackmailed or
otherwise threatened to do so.

"So how do you come to be involved in this matter?" Mr. Pollock asked as he crossed to a beverage cart
and picked up a carafe of brandy. He held it up in
silent question to Branstoke.

"Yes, thank you. I've spent too long in the saddle today." He shifted position in the chair, crossing one booted leg over the other. " —I own the neighboring estate to Lord Aldrich, and my wife is a close friend of Lady Aldrich."

Mr. Pollock frowned. "I have some familiarity with the area. I don't recall—"

"I recently purchased Summerworth Park," James explained.

"Ah, one of the Earl of Morchant's estates."

"One of his unentailed estates that came to him through his mother."

"Of course, of course. Hmm, if I had known he was amenable to selling, I would have made him an offer myself. Excellent piece of land at the edge of the downs."

For some reason that James could not identify, the magistrate's manner irritated him. Maybe this was what Mr. Tinsley had meant by him being a talkative gentleman. However, James didn't think so. The man was probing for something, but James couldn't think what that could be.

"Morchant offered it to me because we are cousins and he thought to keep the property in the family."

"Oh, of course, of course," said the magistrate. He leaned back again as he picked up his brandy glass. His expression made James feel as if he had just dissected him and set him in a specimen jar on his bookshelf.

"But tell me, Sir James, how well do you know Lord Aldrich?"

"Hardly at all. I only know him in passing at the London clubs. He was already gone from Bartlett Hall when we took residence nearby."

Pollock raised his chin as he looked up at the

ceiling in a contemplative manner. "He always struck me as a congenial fellow."

James nodded. "He enjoyed himself, that is certain."

"Would you say he perhaps exhibited a trifle foolishness in his decisions?"

Branstoke studied Pollock over the rim of his brandy glass. He could not understand the direction of Mr. Pollock's questions, and he'd wager there was a direction.

James smiled slightly and inclined his head. "I did not pay attention to him or his cronies in London, so I cannot say."

Mr. Pollock gave a bark of laughter. "I understand. I have another question," he said, sitting up straight and leaning his elbows on the desk. "Do you know a Mr. Melville?"

James raised one eyebrow. "I have met the man," he drawled.

Mr. Pollock laughed again. "Bit of a top-lofty puppy. Came to me asking questions about Lord Aldrich and demanded I surrender the portmanteau to him. Said it was government business."

James frowned. "Did you surrender the portmanteau to him?"

"I did not. I did not like his manner and I knew from your man that you and Lady Aldrich were traveling down here."

James nodded. "I think your description of Captain Melville as a top-lofty puppy is appropriate."

"Captain, you say?" asked Mr. Pollock, his expression intrigued.

"When I met him at Bartlett Hall, I guessed he was military. I called him Lieutenant. He took offense and corrected me, else I don't think we would have admitted the military connection."

"He visited Aldrich's house? When was this?"

"He arrived shortly after Lady Aldrich received your letter. Whilst she was in the throes of grief. He stood before her, asking about her husband's papers, without consideration for Lady Aldrich's feelings. Lady Branstoke and I arrived at this time and sent him on his way. I told him I would endeavor to assist him if he could tell me what his interest was. He would not. We have stayed close to Lady Aldrich as we feared he might pester her."

"Why have you taken an interest in this matter?" asked Mr. Pollock.

"Lady Aldrich is alone, and she is my wife's friend." He smiled. "My lady wife's appearance is deceiving," he explained. "Though small and slender in stature, she has the heart of a lion and would lead a regiment into battle for those she cares for."

"Interesting," said Mr. Pollock. "And she cares for Lady Aldrich? I have heard rumors of Lady Aldrich's antecedents..."

James' eyes narrowed; his expression shuttered at Pollocks damning words.

Mr. Pollock observed the change in Sir James demeanor and blinked rapidly in surprise. He pursed his lips and rapped the desk twice with his fingertips. Then, being an intelligent and cunning man, he let the rest of what he would have said float away between them.

James inclined his head slightly in recognition of the change in conversation direction. He took up the conversation: "Your letter to me, and the one you wrote Lady Aldrich, has led me to a suspicion that

Lord Aldrich is more alive than dead. It's the *What has he gotten into?* question that intrigues me."

Mr. Pollock nodded understanding. "I, on the other hand, do not believe he is alive. He just wasn't killed in the carriage. The carriage is a ruse to forestall the search for a peer. The ruse only failed because where the carriage went over the cliff edge does not fall straight to the sea where tides would remove bodies and therefore support the notion of death," he said.

"There are local smugglers?" James asked.

"Yes, though smugglers are not as prevalent here as they are in other parts of England, they exist here. The proximity to France is too close to ignore. When Napoleon was sent to Elba, the smuggling increased locally. Even though he has escaped, the renewed smuggling hasn't ceased."

"Tinsley advised me not to ride back to the inn tonight. He said it wouldn't be safe."

Mr. Pollock nodded. He appeared pleased that others had advised Sir James as he would. "He told you true," he said with a shrug. "I wish I, in my role as magistrate, could tell you otherwise."

James stared at him for a moment, then nodded slightly. "I have taken a room at The Hound and Hare for the night."

"Excellent."

"So," James said, "will you surrender Lord Aldrich's portmanteau to me?"

Pollock nodded. "I will."

"I assume you have searched the bag and found nothing untoward?" James said.

Pollock sighed. "Only clean linen and a pair of breeches."

"Odd. He has been away from Bartlett Hall for over three weeks."

"Oh, there is one other thing." Mr. Pollock opened a desk drawer and pulled out a letter. "This was also in the portmanteau, addressed to Lady Aldrich and ready to be posted." He pushed it across the desk to James.

James reached for the letter. The seal was broken. "You read it?" he asked.

"Yes." He waved a hand negligently. "Nothing of import. It is just the kind of letter you would expect a husband to send his bride. I did not mention it to Mr.– er *Captain* Melville."

"Thank you for that. The Aldriches are recently married, and Lady Aldrich cares deeply for her husband. I am sure this letter will be a comfort to her," James told the magistrate as he put the letter in his pocket.

"You will not read it?" Pollock asked.

"No, not without permission. You say it is a personal letter. That is all I need to know."

"Ah," said Pollock. "You are an unusual man."

James raised one eyebrow in silent inquiry. Mr. Pollock laughed and shook his head. "Another time, sir. Another time." He rang the bell by his side and immediately his butler opened the door.

"Bernard, see that Sir James' horse is brought around and fetch the portmanteau we collected from the carriage accident. He will take it with him."

"Yes, sir," the man said, bowing himself out of the room.

"Please take the portmanteau with my good will and give my condolences to Lady Aldrich."

5

"I think this was a good idea of Sir James to have us stay together," Elinor said as she brushed her hair. "This way my mind is not stuck reviewing the vision of that carriage down the cliff. Being with you eases the sick feeling in the pit of my stomach."

Cecilia smiled as she laid her brush down and plaited her hair for the night. "It is certainly far easier for us to assist each other when we are in the same room. I admit I didn't think about the help needed to get into or out of our gowns. I think I shall challenge my modiste to design dresses that don't require the assistance of a maid."

"I think a village seamstress would have a much better ability in that area. London fashions can be quite restricting."

"Agreed." Cecilia pulled back the coverlet on her side of the bed, sat down and swung her legs under the covers. "Only think of the jackets for men that are in fashion. They can't be put on without help!"

"Simon has one jacket like that, but he seldom wears it. He ordered it because, between them, Cavanaugh, Simon's valet, and his London tailor convinced him it was all the crack," Elinor said.

She finished plaiting her hair, then crossed to the mantel to blow out the candles there. The only candle remaining burned on a small table on Cecilia's side of the bed. "I did not know that inns outside London could have rooms like this. It is so large!" Elinor said as she climbed into bed. "There is enough room in this one room to make two rooms for travelers!"

Cecilia laughed softly before blowing out the candle. "Good night, Elinor."

"Good night, Cecilia," Elinor said with a yawn.

THE BANKED FIRE in the hearth glowed, casting soft light in the room. Cecilia lay on her side in the enveloping feather mattress. The quilt kept the room's chill out and she felt warm and comfortable. She should have been drowsing off to sleep as Elinor had; however, her mind turned to thoughts of her husband and wondering how his visit went with the magistrate. What was in the portmanteau? What had the magistrate found, or what did he know? Why was the shaft partially sawed? Where was Lord Aldrich? What did that captain want? What did he know? What would happen to Lady Aldrich?

Question upon question chasing each other in her mind kept sleep at bay despite her fatigue.

This was the first night since she married James that they had not shared a bed. Sometimes she could not believe how they had come together, or why he had taken an interest in the flibbertigibbet she had presented to the world.

With a footstep and the creak of a floorboard outside their room, Cecilia's eyes opened. Without moving, she looked across the room to the door. Though dark in the hall, she saw the darker shadow of a man's feet beneath the door. Did James not stay in Folkestone for the night? Or did he set John Coachman to watch over them? Or was someone else outside? Aldrich?

Now she was not acting the flibbertigibbet, she was being one! she chided herself. She quietly reached for the candlestick on the table at her side. She removed the candle, picked up the heavy brass candlestick, and carefully brought it under the covers, her fingers clenched about it.

The window on the far side of the bed let in scudding moonlight as the clouds moved in the night wind. One moment, a shaft of moonlight illuminated the room, and in the next, the clouds plunged it into darkness.

Cecilia heard the door latch lift.

Daphne had suggested they not bar the door so the maid could come in early to stoke their fire and exchange the chamber pots. Now Cecilia realized the foolishness of their acquiescence.

The door quietly swung open, and the silhouette of a man stood in the doorway, much like the silhouettes her aunt Jessamine enjoyed cutting for ton amusement. She noted the man's outline: small-brimmed hat, scraggly longish hair and ill-fitting coat.

This was not her husband, John Coachman, or an inn servant.

Cecilia leaped out of bed, screaming, brandishing the candlestick in front of her. "Get out! Out!" she yelled. "What do you want? Who are you? Get out of here!" Her words tumbled out of her without connection or thought of receiving an answer.

Elinor screamed as well, pulling herself into a ball against the headboard.

Cecilia ran forward, swinging the candlestick at the man. He dodged her, but she managed to graze his arm.

Outside the room, she heard men yelling and boots thundering up the stairs. Elinor continued to scream in short, staccato bursts, her head bobbing up and down to see what was happening, then hiding her face in her arms. Cecilia raised the candlestick again. The man ran across the room to the window, shoving his shoulder against it. Cecilia threw the candlestick at him as the window flew open with a shattering of glass. He rolled out the window onto the porch roof. Cecilia ran to the window to look out as Mr. Tinsley, John Coachman, and Captain Melville burst into the room.

"He's running across the yard!" Cecilia yelled.

John Coachman tripped over Captain Melville's foot as he turned to go in pursuit. He gathered himself up and ran down the hall to the stairs.

Elinor stopped screaming, but drew the quilts up higher around her.

Cecilia rounded on Mr. Tinsley. "Didn't you tell Sir James that we would be safe here? Didn't you tell you would look out for us? How did that man get up here?"

"My lady—" Mr. Tinsley began.

She turned away from him to glare at Captain Melville. "And what are you doing here? Are you following us?"

"I still must speak to Lady Aldrich. It is a matter of national importance," he said as he took a step toward her.

"Aargh! How many times do we have to hear that from you? You are nothing but a—a bounder!" Cecilia cried out. She bent down to retrieve the candlestick from where it had fallen by the window. She brandished it before her. "Get! Out!"

Mr. Tinsley looked from Cecilia to the man. "You should leave, sir," he said, raising his hand in the door's direction.

Melville turned toward Lady Aldrich. "Lady Aldrich, please let me speak to you in private. I can help you."

Silently, she shook her head *no*.

"Sir, I must insist," Mr. Tinsley said, drawing himself up. He stepped in front of Melville and once again gestured his hand toward the door.

"Help?" Cecilia said as she lowered the candlestick. "Why does she need help? What is going on?"

"I cannot answer that," he said stiffly.

"A bounder two times over! Mr. Tinsley, please see him out of this room, and if I were you, I'd see him off your property as well!"

"Sir—"

"I'm leaving," Melville grouched. He turned to stalk out of the room just as John Coachman climbed the stairs.

"Milady," he said from the doorway, "he got away. I couldna' find him."

"He had a good start on you. I wouldn't be surprised if Captain Melville didn't trip you on purpose," Cecilia said caustically.

Mr. Tinsley's eyes widened. "Truly, my lady?" he asked.

Cecilia shook her head. "I don't know," she said. "I just don't trust a man that secretive yet adamant at the same time."

"I'll sleep outside your door all night," John Coachman said. "No one will get past me," he finished grimly.

"I'll have a pallet made up for you," Mr. Tinsley said, addressing John Coachman. "And I'll have a man stay in the taproom below to keep watch." He turned back to Cecilia. "I'll have someone board up the window. There is a small parlor on this floor; you ladies could stay in there while the work is done. I shall have a fire laid in the room and then have my daughter escort you there and serve you some sherry to help settle your nerves."

"Thank you," Cecilia said. "My nerves are quite overwrought. I don't know how I could have thought to confront the man." She shuddered. "Oh dear, I must sit down," she said. "I feel quite faint," she finished weakly.

Elinor looked at her in surprise.

Cecilia sat on the edge of the bed near Elinor and turned her head toward her, flashing a brief grin at her before slumping and turning back to face the innkeeper. "Perhaps a biscuit with the sherry might be good, as well," she said, looking up at Mr. Tinsley.

"Yes, of course, my lady. All will be attended to. I can see how the events of this night might have shattered your sensibilities. But you did very well earlier, very well indeed, and so I shall tell Sir Branstoke."

"Thank you," Cecilia murmured faintly as the man briskly turned to leave the room and close the door behind himself.

"Oh, gracious, Cecilia, is that how you feinted illness in London? I swear you could tread the boards better than any actress I have seen."

"I shall have to keep it up for the rest of our stay here. I want to ensure the innkeeper feels increasingly guilty and therefore highly attentive to all that goes on. I would like to know that he sends the captain on his way; however, he won't get coin from that room

Melville's rented this late, so I can't see him turning the captain out."

"Especially if Captain Melville is involved in something important for the government," Elinor added. "Our proprietor will walk a fine line to protect his business."

"True." Cecilia rose from the bed. "We'd best put our shawls about us. I, for one, did not bring a dressing gown. At least I do have slippers."

Cecilia picked up Elinor's fine wool, purple and tan plaid shawl and handed it to her before gathering up her blue and green Indian paisley shawl. Their shawls were large and fell to the back of their legs and could be wrapped warmly and modestly about their bodies.

By the time Daphne knocked on their door to escort them to the parlor, Cecilia had told Elinor how to minister to her so it would seem she was conversant with Cecilia's health issues. Cecilia leaned on Elinor as they followed Daphne to the small parlor. A fire blazed in the grate, and a carafe of sherry and two glasses sat on a tray in the middle of the table.

"Here you go, m'ladies. Stephen should be able to board up that window in no time, but rest here and I'll be back to fetch you when he's done."

"Thank you," Elinor said, as she escorted Cecilia to a chair and poured her a glass of sherry.

Daphne bobbed a curtsy and left them alone.

"ELINOR, I think Captain Melville deliberately tripped John Coachman. He wanted that man to get away," Cecilia said as she stared at the fire in the grate.

"Oh, no, Cecilia, surely not!" exclaimed Elinor. "Why should he do that?"

"I don't know. And how did he get to our room so soon? I wonder if Mr. Tinsley put him in the room you were in earlier? The one James already paid for," she mused.

"Surely not!"

Cecilia laughed. "No matter. James shall sort it out when he returns. But I do wonder what papers he thinks Lord Aldrich might have that would interest the government."

"We didn't receive any letters save for the packet from the solicitor regarding the marriage portion. We did, however, have a visitor, about a week before Simon went away."

"Who was that?" Cecilia asked.

"Lord Wheaten, an older gentleman. He traveled in what I took to be an ancient Berlin carriage and was accompanied by his valet. Said he'd come from London and was on his way to Dover."

"Do you think he might have given Lord Aldrich some papers?"

"I couldn't say. They spent long hours in the library; I do not know what they may have discussed or done. They could have just been reading or blowing a cloud. But otherwise, he was a kindly gentleman and a pleasant dinner companion. He has a deep interest in the welfare of our veterans. And now that Napoleon has escaped Elba, he says government funds to support veterans will be diverted to a renewed war effort."

Cecilia sighed. "He's probably right, though I don't think the government thinks about the veterans at all! If they did, there would not be so many begging in London." She frowned. "How long did he stay?"

"Two nights."

"Hmm. I admit, I don't know the name; however, I wager James shall. I shall mention this to James. What did he look like?"

"Slender, middling height, I'd say. He had a very slight stoop. His eyes were brown—a friendly brown, if you know what I mean. Stringy brown hair liberally streaked with gray and tied at his neck in the old queue style. His clothes were well made, not worn-looking, but a little out of style."

A quick knock on the door preceded Daphne's entrance.

"M'ladies, your room is ready."

"That was quick!" observed Elinor.

Daphne smiled and bobbed a curtsy. "Yes, m'lady. I told Stephen if he knew what was good for him, he'd make haste."

"But did he do a good job in his haste?"

"Oh, yes, m'lady. Me da checked it, as did your coachman."

Cecilia finished her sherry and returned the small cordial glass to the tray.

"Shall I bring the sherry to your room?" Daphne asked.

Cecilia exchanged glances with Elinor, and they both grinned like naughty little girls. Cecilia turned back to Daphne. "I think that is an excellent idea."

Still smiling, the ladies left the parlor and headed down the hall to their room. The only thing that marred Cecilia's good humor was looking down the open stairway and seeing Captain Melville on the ground floor enjoying a pint of ale with John Coachman.

6

When Cecilia opened the door to their room in the morning, she discovered John Coachman snoring from his pallet on the wood floor in front of their door. She reached down and touched his shoulder. That worthy bolted awake, arms flailing. Cecilia quickly stepped back, out of harm's way, while suppressing a laugh at the way the big man woke up.

John Coachman scrambled to his feet. "Pardon, m'lady," he said, tugging on his forelock.

"Too many pints last night?" she asked, still annoyed that she'd seen him with Melville.

He bent to pick up his hat from the floor and settle it on his head. "Maybe a mite," he confessed, ducking his head and looking down.

"With Captain Melville," she stated repressively.

"Yes, m'lady," he said meekly. Then he looked up at her. "'Twere obvious he wasn't leavin', so figured best to keep him in sight. Might learn a bit fer Sir James," he said earnestly.

"And did you?"

He flushed. "No, m'lady, that one's a tight mouth, fer sure."

Cecilia sighed, letting her annoyance go. "Go

break your fast, then check on the horses. I'm sure Sir James will want to leave today, as do I and Lady Aldrich."

"Yes, m'lady." He gathered up the pallet and headed for the stairway.

"What was that about?" Elinor asked Cecilia, coming up beside her.

She turned toward her. "When we returned to our room last night, I chanced to look down the staircase and saw Captain Melville and John Coachman quite convivial together," she said. She closed the room door. "He tells me that was his way of monitoring the gentleman since he wasn't leaving this establishment."

"That does make sense, Cecilia," Elinor said.

Cecilia knew it made sense, perhaps the only thing that did. Nonetheless, she felt unsettled. Strange men breaking into an inn room where two women slept just did not happen. "I wonder if they found any sign of our intruder, or if anyone looked further," she finished caustically.

"What are you thinking?"

"I'm uncertain that I even know what I am thinking right now! It all seemed just a little too convenient. So many possibilities. Most likely I am borrowing trouble with my thoughts." She sat down on the edge of the bed.

Elinor sat down beside her. "Best to think of the possibilities and probabilities and to discard the outlandish ideas as it is to be surprised," she advised.

"There is that, I suppose." She looked at the boarded-up window, then looked about the room as if seeing it for the first time. She slapped her hands on her knees and resolutely stood up again, shelving aside her errant, wayward, and unfocused thoughts. "I wonder if we might have breakfast in that little private parlor we were in last night. I, for one, do not wish to chance running into Captain Melville. I should be much too irritated to feint illness to him."

Elinor rose as well. "Let's see if anyone is in there before us and if not, just claim it," Elinor suggested with a shrug. She passed Cecilia her shawl, then grabbed her own.

Cecilia laughed despite her unsettled thoughts. "I do like the way you think. It is no wonder I like you."

Elinor smiled. "And I you, as well," she said, taking Cecilia's arm in hers as she opened the room door and led Cecilia toward the parlor.

A disturbance from below halted them. They looked over the railing to the pub room below.

"James!" Cecilia exclaimed, seeing her husband cross the room toward the innkeeper. He'd obviously just returned as he still wore his greatcoat and hat. Pulling her arm free from Elinor, she hurried down the stairs. She wanted to warn James not to speak to Mr. Tinsley yet, and she knew just how to do so.

"Oh, James, I am so happy to see you. You cannot know how my heart has pounded so with you away. We have had such a fright!" she cried out. "And me, away from home without my lavender water."

Branstoke's eyes widened infinitesimally, then returned to their habitual heavy-lidded gaze. He casually raised her hand to his lips. "I am here now, my love."

"Mr. Tinsley," called Elinor down over the railing. "Might we have breakfast in the private parlor?"

"Yes, yes, at once," he said. He looked at Branstoke. "Might I have a word with you in private, Sir James?"

Branstoke felt Cecilia's slight head shake from where it rested on his chest.

"Later. First, I must attend to my lovely wife," he said, guiding Cecilia to the stairs.

Cecilia made to lean heavily on his arm as they approached the stairs, then squeaked when Branstoke lifted her up in his arms to carry her. Above, Elinor giggled.

"James!" Cecilia protested softly.

"I am merely following your stage direction," he whispered, smiling down at her.

AFTER BREAKFAST HAD BEEN SERVED and the inn servant had bowed out of the room, Cecilia shed her fainting pose and sat up. "James, you will not believe who is staying here at the inn."

"Captain Melville," he said calmly, before placing a rasher of bacon on his plate.

"Oh, blast it!" she exclaimed.

Branstoke raised an eyebrow at his wife's language.

"You are always so percipient," she complained.

"Not always," he murmured, thinking of the time he had almost lost her to human trafficking. His gut clenched at the memory.

"But how did you know?" interjected Elinor. She set her teacup on the table and picked up a roll. Cecilia pushed the jam pot in her direction.

James finished buttering his toast as he dismissed his memories. He looked up. "When I arrived at the magistrate's residence, I discovered Captain Melville had already been to see him. He requested he be given the portmanteau Mr. Pollock mentioned in his note to you, Elinor."

"Did he give it to him?" she asked.

"No, luckily, he did not, as I had written that I

would come for it on your behalf," James assured her before taking a bite of his toast.

"That still doesn't explain how you concluded Captain Melville would be here," Cecilia said.

James took a sip of coffee. "Where else could he be? This is the nearest inn to the site of the carriage accident. Somehow, I can't envision Captain Melville roughing it. But, come, Cecilia, tell me what spurred the play you enacted, and how it involves Captain Melville."

"All right." She took a deep breath, marshalling her emotions and memories from the previous night.

"I was slow to fall asleep. As my side of the bed was closest to the door, at the bottom of the door I could see a dim light from the outside hall. I was drowsing when something caused me to become alert. There was a shadow across part of the bottom of the door. Then I heard the soft lifting of the door latch. I grabbed the heavy brass candlestick from beside me. As the door opened, I leaped out of bed, screamed, and tried to hit the intruder with the candlestick. The man ran for the window. With his shoulder, he burst through the window and leaped out. He went over the porch roof. Just then, Mr. Tinsley, Captain Melville and John Coachman burst into the room. I told them an intruder had gone out the window. John Coachman turned to catch him, but he fell over the captain's foot. I don't doubt the captain deliberately tripped him to slow him down."

James felt a cold hand clutch at his heart, but refused to react to it. Instead, he looked at Elinor for confirmation.

"I saw nothing; I was too busy screaming," Elinor stated matter-of-factly, but with a glint in her eyes.

James laughed, letting the tension that had gathered within him dissipate. It was over and done. They were safe. "Well said, Elinor. Well said," he acknowledged with a wry smile. "But now I must be serious." He reached into his pocket and drew out a folder letter. "Mr. Pollock fund this in the portmanteau. It is addressed to you."

"From Simon?" Her eyes grew round. She snatched the letter from his hand. "The seal is broken. Have you read it?"

He shook his head. "No, I have not. Mr. Pollock did. He said it was personal. He also said he did not mention the existence of the letter to Captain Melville."

Elinor's fingers trembled as she unfolded the paper to read the letter.

A hand rose to finger the fichu at her neck as she read. By her shifting expressions, the Branstokes knew something was wrong.

"I don't understand!" she exclaimed, laying the letter on the table before her. She waved her hand at the document. "This is in Simon's hand, that I can attest, but the letter makes no sense! None at all!"

"May we read it?" Cecilia asked, extending her hand.

"Please," Elinor said, pushing it toward Cecilia. "It is a puzzle to me, or did he mean to write this to another lady?"

Cecilia glanced down at the letter, then back up at Elinor. "I doubt that; it starts out with: *My dearest wife.*"

James rose from his chair and came around the table to read over Cecilia's shoulder.

My dearest wife,
It is late and I am more tired than usual. I conclude it is

too much salt sea air. But I must answer your letter before I sleep. Your questions prey upon my mind.

No. Do not go to Margate. I was there—briefly last June, before spending 8 days at Penwick Park. It was a rackety place. Entirely unsuitable for a woman in your condition. And before you ask, I shall say the same for Brighton. Choose some place between the two in distance. If the weather turns sultry and too unbearable before I return, ask your folks to go with you. The chalk cliffs are lovely, but be careful you don't turn an ankle walking on the stones.

I have no suggestions for baby names. Ask Kate. She's always interested in familial connections. It was she who suggested Simon.

Regrettably, I cannot recommend a military career for your cousin. He is not officer material. If he insists, he'll have to look elsewhere for his commission money. The Iron Duke will do better without officers of his ilk.

Finally, turn to Mr. Ash on all estate matters. I am aware Mr. Miller feels in command. Such is not the case. When in doubt, you may consult your father.

Your obedient servant,

Simon

"And before you ask, no, I am not with child."

Branstoke straightened. "There is some sort of hidden message in this letter. I wonder if this is what Melville is looking for."

"Do we show it to him?"

Branstoke thought for a moment. "I'm not inclined to," he said. "Mr. Pollock thought Aldrich might have fallen in with smugglers. There was a resurgence of smuggling when Napoleon was sent to Elba, and even though he has now escaped, the smuggling has not decreased. We don't know upon which side of this affair Melville might fall, though I am inclined to think he is wholly Candelstone's minion."

"We should interview Simon's valet. He might know this Kate person," Elinor suggested.

The door opened and Captain Melville entered with an air of urbane entitlement. He came up to the table.

James straightened. "This is a private parlor, sir," he said repressively.

Melville ignored him. "Is that a missive from Lord Aldrich?" he asked, spying the letter in Cecilia's hand. He reached for it.

Cecilia stuffed it down her dress front.

"Captain!" Branstoke said sharply. "You forget yourself!" He moved to stand between Cecilia and the man.

"But... but..." Melville said, moving from side to side, trying to look around Branstoke to the letter's hiding place. "You don't understand!"

James placed his hands on his hips and glared at Melville. "That is correct and we will continue to not understand until you tell us what this is about."

"I cannot. You must understand. I am sworn to secrecy."

"First you say we don't understand and then you say we must understand. Very noble of you, but the least bit forthcoming for us to understand anything you are saying. Let me help you start your explanation. You work for Lord Candelstone."

Melville's eyes flew up to Branstoke's face. "How... No, no, I don't know a Candelstone."

"Your expression and the first word you uttered gave you away." James crossed his arms over his chest. "I have had dealings with another of Candelstone's agents and his secrecy almost cost Lady Branstoke her freedom. Here is what *you* must understand. I have no patience for Candelstone and his games."

Melville sank down into the chair Branstoke had vacated to read the letter. He ran a hand through his blond hair and sighed heavily. He looked like a frustrated schoolboy. "In truth, I don't know. My task is to get any correspondence from or to Lord Aldrich, by any means."

"Like last night hiring a man to break into the room where the ladies were sleeping?"

"What?" Elinor gasped. She and Cecilia stared at the man.

"Yes, but they were always safe. He wasn't going to do them any harm. I was to come to their rescue, and he was to escape through the window, as he did. We had it all planned out. Then Lady Branstoke started screaming, and Lady Aldrich screamed, and there was a big rush to get to them. Tinsley and your coachman pushed me aside as I was about to open the door to rescue them. That wasn't how it was supposed to happen."

"So you did trip John Coachman as he made to chase after the intruder."

"Yes."

Cecilia looked up at her husband. "This sounds like one of Lord Candelstone's intrigues," she said, disgusted.

Melville looked from one to the other. "What do you mean? How do you know Lord Candelstone?"

"Did you read in the papers about the ship burning in the harbor earlier this spring? That could have been prevented if Candelstone hadn't been so secretive."

"How does any of this relate to Simon? What is this all about? Is my husband dead?"

Branstoke looked at Melville.

"I—I don't know, my lady," he said wretchedly.

Branstoke stared at him a moment through hooded eyes, then turned back to Elinor.

"I would venture to—guardedly—say no. That is not to say it may not still occur."

"No!" exclaimed Elinor.

Cecilia reached across the table to squeeze her hand reassuringly.

"If this is another of Candelstone's investigations, I'd wager Lord Aldrich is working undercover," Cecilia said.

"That appears to be the type of modus operandi he engages in. It is what Lord Havelock was engaged in, and what Lord Blessingame, Captain Melville's brother-in-law, did that got him killed," James said.

"How do you know all this?" Melville asked, incredulous.

"I believe when we met I told you I was a friend of Lady Blessingame."

"Isabella told you?" Melville exclaimed.

"She was distraught," James said. He sighed. "What Candelstone cannot appreciate is people have emotions. Most likely because he does not have any. He does not appreciate that a wife might mourn and want answers when a man's death is suspect. They made no effort to provide Lady Blessingame with information, or concoct a cover story, or otherwise deal with her as the widow or a member of his own network. Consequently, your sister did her own investigation, for which she came to me for advice."

Melville nodded and straightened in his chair. "May I see the letter?" he said in a calmer tone. "Maybe there is something in it that relates to what little Candelstone has told me."

Branstoke considered for a moment, then turned to his wife. "Cecilia, please allow Captain Melville to read the letter."

"Do you think that is wise?"

"As he is one of Candelstone's minions, yes, it seems we should. As much as I dislike Candelstone, he does work for the government. And I don't know how he does it; however, Candelstone engenders a fierce loyalty in his puppets."

Melville bristled. "I am not a puppet!"

"Then stop acting as one," bit out James.

Cecilia withdrew the crumbled letter from the top of her dress and slowly extended it to Captain Melville.

Melville snatched it from her and twisted to escape with the letter in hand. Expecting his action, James was before him, leaning back against the door. Melville tried to push him aside to get out with his prize. James grabbed his arm and swung him backward. Melville fell against the wall, but quickly got up and charged James, only to be met with a powerful right hook that sent him to the floor.

"Well done, James!" Cecilia said, delighted.

James inclined his head toward her and then he bent over and took the letter from Melville. He shook his head as he stared down at him. "Idiocy. Sheer idiocy. We agree to let you see the letter and this is what you do." He handed the letter to Elinor, then brushed off the sleeves of his jacket. "I shall be in London in two days," he informed Melville, his manner drawling. "Tell Candelstone he can come to my home if he wishes to see the letter. We are not playing with you. Now get out."

Melville swiped at blood on his lip with the back of his hand. "Lord Candelstone will not like this."

"I'm sure he won't," James said, his voice leaching boredom.

Melville struggled to his feet, then left the room.

"That is twice now that our host has failed in his commitment to me. I wonder what I should take from that," James mused. He picked up his coffee mug to take a drink, but set it down again when he realized it had gone cold. He looked at Cecilia and Elinor.

"Elinor, I suggest you stay with Cecilia at Summerworth Park while I make inquiries in London and meet with Lord Candelstone."

"James, I will not be left behind."

"Nor I."

Branstoke looked severely at the women. "This is not—"

"If you don't take us with you, we shall follow behind," Cecilia threatened.

Branstoke knew hers was not an idle threat, but he wasn't about to acquiesce so easily. "We will discuss this after we meet with Lord Aldrich's valet. Gather your things. I'll have Mr. Tinsley come to get them. We leave for Summerworth Park in half an hour."

7

"I'm sorry, my lady, I don't understand this letter either," Cavanaugh, Lord Aldrich's valet, said, shaking his head. Confusion wrinkled the man's forehead.

They were back in the library at Bartlett Hall. Elinor sat behind the desk, with Cecilia to her right. The afternoon sun sent shafts of light across the room. The room was too bright for candles, yet too dark for an intense search. They had been going through desk drawers, tapping for any hidden spaces, and carefully reviewing every scrap of paper they found when Mr. Cavanaugh entered. They invited him to sit in the other chair at the desk and read the letter. Reluctantly he sat, then squirmed in the chair, apparently uncomfortable with two pairs of female eyes studying him.

"That is his hand..." He trailed off, setting the paper on the scarred and scratched desk surface.

Elinor sighed deeply as she looked at Cecilia.

Cecilia pursed her lips. "We know it is. What about the Kate person he mentions?" she asked.

Cavanaugh hesitated, glancing nervously about. He looked like a rabbit trying to decide which way to bolt.

Cecilia slapped the flat of her hand on the desk. "You do know!" she said. "I can tell by your expression," she said triumphantly, leaning forward.

Cavanaugh blinked and pressed back against the chair, he appeared afraid Cecilia would pounce on him.

"Cavanaugh, if you have any idea, you must tell us," said Elinor softly but urgently.

The man squirmed in his chair and wouldn't meet her gaze.

"Is this Kate his mistress?" Elinor asked. "Do not be afraid. I am aware of Aldrich's reputation. I did not go into my marriage naïve as to the ways of society men," she said ruefully.

Cavanaugh took a deep breath and finally looked up at her. "Lord Aldrich had a mistress named Kate. I believe he ended the association before his marriage to you."

"But you don't know for certain," Cecilia prodded.

Cavanaugh looked down again. "No, my lady," he said softly, then looked up again. "But if I may be a bit forward, my lady. He had seemed much happier in marriage."

Elinor smiled at the uncomfortable, miserable man. "Thank you for that, Mr. Cavanaugh. Now, one more thing, do you know this woman's name and direction?" she asked gently, striving to leave the man with some masculine dignity before two inquisitive ladies.

"*Sinclair*," he intoned, his hands wrapped tightly about the chair arms. "Her last name is Sinclair."

"Excellent," Elinor said, leaning back slightly. "And—"

The door to the library opened to admit James. "So what unfortunate are you grilling before my arrival?" he asked with good-natured, but pointed humor.

Cavanaugh surged to his feet, running a hand across his balding pate to smooth any wayward hairs.

Elinor and Cecilia exchanged guilty looks.

"Cavanaugh, sir. William Cavanaugh."

"Ah, Lord Aldrich's man." James looked at his wife. "It would have been preferred that you await my arrival."

"But, James," Cecilia began while Elinor guiltily looked to the side.

James held up a hand to forestall her. "No matter. I am here now." He crossed the room to the desk where they gathered. "Sit, Mr. Cavanaugh," he invited, while he sat on a corner of the desk. "Now continue what you were saying to Lady Aldrich and Lady Branstoke."

Cavanaugh sank down on the edge of the chair. "Not much more to say, sir. I know Miss Sinclair was an actress. I don't know the woman's address, but I suspect it was not far from Aldrich House as he could go and return in less than an hour." He paused a moment, a troubled frown pulling his features together. "Now that I think on it, she may not be in that area now. I recall Lord Aldrich saying something about letting his other town property go."

"Gave her the go bye, did he?" Cecilia said.

"Cecilia!" her husband remonstrated her with a laugh.

She looked up at him and shrugged. "Well, if true, that makes me feel better toward Lord Aldrich."

"I think it is true," said Elinor with a wistful smile.

"Faugh! But it would be so much easier to have her direction," Cecilia said petulantly.

James laughed. He reached forward to brush a strand of hair that had fallen out of her chignon back behind her ear. "I trust Mr. Thornbridge to find her direction easily enough."

"Yes, true," Cecilia said, nodding.

"So, Mr. Cavanaugh, what can you tell us about Lord Aldrich's cronies? Who were his associates?"

"Lord Aldrich didn't have close friends. He liked to be friends with everyone." Cavanaugh paused and scratched the side of his nose. "I suppose Misters Bourneway and Sedgwick might be the closest to steady friends."

"I believe I was introduced to those gentlemen at our wedding," Elinor put in. "They seemed to be all that is polite and amiable."

"I know the men slightly," James said. "Rackety, by harmless enough."

"So what of this Lord Wheaten Elinor told me of, who spent a couple of nights here?" Cecilia asked.

"Wheaten!" Branstoke exclaimed. He looked from Cecilia to Elinor. "You never told me about Wheaten."

"Sorry, James, Elinor told me at the inn and with all going on and the letter, I forgot about him," Cecilia said with a contrite smile.

"I wonder what Aldrich could be doing with Wheaten as a friend," James mused. "That is an interesting wrinkle."

"Why is that?" Cecilia asked.

"Wheaten sees himself as a bit of a radical. I believe his intentions are generally good; however, his execution, er—lacks," he said drily. "He writes diatribes about the cost of war and how that money is better spent in the country on our poor, has them printed up, then reads his little pamphlets loudly from street corners in the city."

"Gracious!" Elinor exclaimed. "That does not sound like anyone Simon would associate with, nor does it sound like the man who came to stay with us a couple nights." She laughed. "Doubtless he was on his best behavior."

"You wouldn't know it to look at him or to hear him talk, but the man is rich as Croesus," James said. "And as far as I have heard, he's not given a tuppence to any charity; he just harangues the government to do so."

"He spoke enthusiastically on the needs of the poor, when he was here. I liked the little man. He was eccentric but quite personable in an old-fashioned, charming way," Elinor said.

"Lord Aldrich likes to be liked, and a friend to all. No doubt Wheaten imposed on your husband's good nature when he stopped here. If Wheaten could have free lodging, free food, and be able to rest his cattle, he'd take advantage of that, nipfarthing that he is," James said.

"Lord Aldrich said as much to me when Lord Wheaten sent round the letter saying he would stop here," Cavanaugh said. "He laughed about it. Didn't seem offended nor bothered."

"Thank you, Cavanaugh," Elinor said. "If you can think of any other names, I'd appreciate hearing them."

Cavanaugh rose to leave.

"One last thing, Cavanaugh, before you leave," James said. "What was Aldrich's manner before he left? Did he say he might be away for more than a couple days?"

Cavanaugh frowned as he shook his head. "No, sir, else he would have taken me. He likes his clean linens and his cravats tied just so."

James nodded. "Such is my thought on Aldrich as well. Thank you for answering our questions."

Cavanaugh bowed and let himself out of the library. James slid off the corner of the desk and took the seat Cavanaugh vacated, his legs sprawled out in front of him. It was an uncommon posture for James, a man typically aware of his appearance before others.

"This morning I sent a follow-up letter to Mr. Pollock about the events at the inn. I wrote to Thornbridge to set him on the scent for answers for us, and to the housekeeper and butler at the London house to expect us tomorrow. Will you be ready to remove yourself and your immediate servants to London tomorrow, Elinor?"

"I believe so. I will need to check with my groomsmen about the horses and carriages."

James nodded. "If there is a problem, let me know and we will procure additional horseflesh from the inn in the village. I assume you will want to stay the night here rather than with us at Summerworth Park? I can understand it; however, it causes me some concern. I have arranged to have a couple of my staff join yours to make sure there is a safe watch kept through the night. We don't want any repeats of Melville's behavior."

"I'm sure that is unnecessary, James, after what happened at The Seagull."

He smiled and stood up. "I'm sure you are. Humor me, please," James said as he left the library.

Elinor turned to Cecilia. "Is he always so managing?"

Cecilia laughed freely and smiled after her husband. "No, sometimes he's worse!" she confided.

THEY MADE excellent time on their journey to London. It was just approaching the noon hour when the carriage pulled up before the Branstoke townhouse.

While Cecilia had not spent more than one night in the house before—and that her wedding night— she felt happy to return to the house for its memories.

It was an older townhouse off Berkley Square, dark stucco over brick that was only two floors above the ground floor. Its biggest draw for James when he acquired the house had been its own mews, so he could stable his horses and carriage. It was a handsome house, though Cecilia was not fond of its black-painted door, far too somber against the charcoal-gray stucco.

The household had been on the watch for them and the minute the carriage stopped, a footman came out the front door to open the carriage door and let down the steps. He handed out first Cecilia, then Elinor. James jumped down after them and, offering both ladies his arms, led them up the steps before the house.

The footman scurried to get before them to open the tall door.

"Welcome home, Lady Branstoke, Sir James," said the butler. He stood off to the side with a silver salver holding a pile of correspondence.

"Thank you, Charwood," James said, reaching for the letters even before he removed his coat and high-crowned beaver hat. He sifted through the collection, then selected one to read.

"Excellent," he murmured on scanning the contents. He shoved the rest of the correspondence in a greatcoat pocket.

"Did you say something, James?" Cecilia asked as she handed her cloak to the footman.

"I shall leave you ladies to freshen up and rest from the journey to London," James said.

Cecilia paused in untying the ribbon of her bonnet. "But we just arrived here! Where are you going?"

"To my club." His eyes flicked to the footman standing beside Cecilia, holding her cloak and waiting to take her bonnet, then back to her.

Cecilia understood he did not want to say more in the presence of staff. Annoyance compressed her lips. "I wish you had said something earlier."

Branstoke smiled, understanding her dismay. "I should have. I am remiss."

"Humph," she said. She looked at him severely. "Will you be back in time for supper?"

"Yes, for I will need to change for our theater outing this evening."

"Theater!" exclaimed Elinor.

Cecilia brightened. "Ah! You hope to speak with Kate Sinclair after the play." She looked at him suspiciously. "And how do you know she is currently in a play?"

"That was one of the questions I sent off to Mr. Thornbridge, yesterday. And I have the answer here," he said, holding up the letter he'd read.

"Excellent. I knew we could count on David Thornbridge. So why are you off to your club?" Cecilia asked.

"I have a friend who won a season box from the Marquis of Kenyon in a friendly card game. I'm going to see if it is available for us this evening. Its location is excellent for viewing the play, as well as the theatergoers."

Cecilia laughed. "You have the wonderful ability to think ahead."

"And you are fortunate that I do," he said.

"I suppose this errand makes up for your traipsing to your club where I cannot go, that bastion of male hideaways," she said with mock woefulness.

He finished removing her bonnet for her and kissed her cheek. "Here is Mrs. Dunstan now to see you upstairs."

She turned to greet the housekeeper. "Hello, Mrs. Dunstan. Elinor, may I make you known to Mrs. Dunstan? She has served Sir James since he purchased the townhouse. Mrs. Dunstan, this is Lady Aldrich, my friend and neighbor in Kent."

Mrs. Dunstan, a tall though spare woman, dipped into a small curtsy.

"I hope this late-notice visit will not put a burden upon you and the staff," Cecilia continued.

"Not at all, your ladyship. Your maids arrived before you and are in your rooms unpacking. I have taken the liberty of directing the kitchen staff to prepare water for hot baths for you. They should bring it up shortly."

"Thank you, Mrs. Dunstan." She turned toward Elinor." –, let's meet in the library an hour before dinner. And please bring the letter with you. After the way Captain Melville behaved, I think we should make copies."

"That is an excellent idea! I shall see you then," Elinor said as she shook out her travel-wrinkled skirts.

THE GRUBBY URCHIN who had followed James since he'd left the London townhouse ran on down the street as he entered White's. He'd seen the lad loitering near his home when they'd arrived; however, he had not thought about the child until he noted him following him as he left the house for a brisk walk to his club. After time spent cramped up in the coach, the walk felt good. The lad practically had to run to keep him in his sights.

He should have changed before coming to the club. Some of the club members would frown on his travel attire. Too bad.

He nodded genially to several members. Seeing the dour Earl of Soothcoor at a table in the corner, he smiled and crossed the room to him.

"Care if I join you?"

Soothcoor looked up and halfway rose to his feet. "Branstoke! Yes! Sit, sit yurself—Thought you were away on yur honeymoon with yur new wife." He pushed strands of lank, black and gray hair away from his face as he sat again.

"I was." He waved to a waiter, then pulled a chair out and sat down at Soothcoor's right. "Coffee," he said to the waiter.

"Coffee?!" Soothcoor exclaimed. "You should have this ale," he said, holding up his tankard.

"Been in a carriage for too many hours. Likely to fall asleep and this day is far from done."

Soothcoor tucked his chin down and stared at James as if he were staring at him over spectacles. "I was wonderin' aboot yur attire. Trouble with the new wife already?"

Branstoke shook his head but refrained from answering until the waiter sat his coffee before him and left.

"How well do you know Lord Aldrich?"

Soothcoor shrugged. "Well enough for a hand a'-cards or sharin' a bootle."

Branstoke nodded. "I have had the same acquaintance."

"So why the question?"

"My wife and Lady Aldrich have become friends. I purchased Summerworth Park from Morchant over a month ago. That is where Lady Branstoke and I have been. It has been severely neglected; we're trying to set it to rights. The property marches Aldrich's Bartlett Park in Kent at the edge of the South Downs."

"Has Aldrich been abusing her ladyship? Wouldna thought that of Aldrich. Sad rattle, but harmless. Newly married himself."

"No, he has not been abusive, except in the concept of he's missing. For over a month now."

"Missing!"

James nodded as he scanned the room. The club was quiet. Only a few gentlemen sat at their leisure, mostly alone, reading one of the newspapers White's subscribed to for its members, or talking softly with another member. With Brummel and Alvanley absent, the bow window seats were empty. They probably had dinner at Watiers. Though White's served meals, Brummel preferred Watiers' food.

"His new wife received an epistle from the Folkestone area magistrate implying Aldrich died in a carriage accident."

Soothcoor furrowed his brow and set his ale down. "What are you saying? You have me all at sea here, as I'm sure you mean to."

"The carriage went over the cliffs between Folkestone and Dover."

"Jest the carriage?"

"Just the carriage. No horses, no bodies, no blood. The horses, in their harness with a partially sawedthrough center shaft, were discovered near the accident."

"Sloppy."

One corner of James' lips kicked up in a wry smile. "Exactly."

"So, young Aldrich faked his death."

James acknowledged that conclusion with a nod. "Possibly, or he is dead, and someone faked the accident to channel questions in a different direction."

Soothcoor cocked his head to the side as he considered James. "What do you think?"

"Lady Aldrich does not believe her husband is dead," James said. He leaned back in his chair. "I tend to agree with her as other events have happened that suggest Aldrich was involved in something over his head. He sent what we can only believe is a coded message to his wife. If the message was meant for her, it failed, as she does not know what the missive could mean. The area magistrate believes Aldrich became involved with local smuggling."

James shrugged his shoulders. "That is a possibility," he continued, "but unlikely. A young military man has been trying to get information on what Aldrich was doing. He went so far as to hire a man to break into Lady Aldrich's room to scare her."

"What?"

James nodded at the irate expression on Soothcoor's face. He continued, "This military sapscull's plan was to come to her rescue and thereby curry favor with her."

"Egad! Is she all right?"

"As fate, and my request would have it, she was sharing the room with my wife. Lady Branstoke scared the intruder away, brandishing, I'm told, a brass candlestick."

Soothcoor shook his head. "And her being such a wee thing."

James smiled. "She does cut up my peace. Rarer than gold, is my wife."

Soothcoor laughed. "She's a right one for you. You needed a mite a shakin' up. Too damned blasé. Nothing phases you."

Branstoke laughed and inclined his head. "Now, ennui no longer visits, and I admit, I do not miss it."

Soothcoor laughed as well, but Branstoke's attention had turned to the doorway. His eyes took on their contemplative, heavy-lidded stare as he noted the person who entered the room. And that person noted him.

Candelstone.

"Ah, so the urchin did—as I thought—have a purpose," Branstoke said softly.

"Pardon?" Soothcoor asked.

He turned back to Soothcoor. "If Candelstone makes his way here to speak to me, do not excuse yourself."

"I gather he be the reason yur in London instead of on yur honeymoon."

Branstoke inclined his head in faint agreement.

Soothcoor smirked.

Lord Candelstone made his way slowly across the room. He was not a tall man, but he possessed a chest shaped like an ale barrel. He tucked his thumbs in his dark blue waistcoat pockets. He walked with consequence, his shoulders back and chin up as he scanned everyone in the room. He was going bald and though he grew sideburns to compensate for losing hair on the top of his head, the remaining fringe of gray-streaked brown hair was neatly trimmed. His eyes were a pale, almost colorless blue, his cheeks a ruddy red. Here was a man who clearly thrived on his own importance.

"Branstoke, Soothcoor," he said when he stopped by their table.

"Would you caire to join us, my lord?" invited Soothcoor, indicating the chair to his left.

"No, thank you," Candelstone replied, barely glancing in Soothcoor's direction, his attention fixed on James. "Branstoke, a word, please."

"I am at your service," James said languidly, bowing his head slightly but otherwise not moving from his chair.

"In private, sir," Candelstone said in a soft, commanding tone that would have sent a subaltern scrambling.

James raised his cup to his lips. "Did Captain Melville not relay my message to you?" he asked, as if that were enough.

"He did," Candelstone admitted.

"I requested you call at my townhouse tomorrow morning," James reminded him.

Candelstone gave him a fulminating look. "I don't believe that will be necessary," he said repressively. "You have merely to send Lord Aldrich's letter to me and—"

"No," James said, cutting him off.

"No?" Candelstone seemed astounded to hear the word.

"That is what I said." He turned to Soothcoor. "That is what I said, did I not?"

"Aye, that you did."

"Ah, I thought so. Thank you." He turned toward Candelstone again. "No," he repeated.

Candelstone's color rose. "This is a matter of national security," he ground out between clenched teeth.

James cocked his head to the side, one long index

finger tapping his chin. "Your Captain Melville said the same thing, but he never provided details. Are you ready to explain yourself?" James asked.

When Candelstone merely compressed his lips, James continued, "You must consider it from my point of view. Lord Aldrich has a reputation as a good-natured rattle. He is not one I would consider being involved in a matter of national security. If you have done so," he said, taking another sip of coffee, "you are no doubt using him as cannon fodder and I cannot like that. He is newly married to a woman who is in love with him."

Candelstone laughed. "In love! Pshaw. Lady Candelstone and I introduced them at a function last year. Theirs was a marriage of convenience."

James shrugged negligently. "Perhaps that is how it started."

Candelstone's brow furrowed. "What is that to mean?"

"It means Lady Aldrich is much attached to her husband and is of a mind to find out where he is. Reminds me of Lady Blessingame. She has the bit between her teeth. You cannot pull on her reins to steer her where you wish her to go."

Candelstone laughed again and appeared to relax. "I had not realized you were so ignorant in the ways of women, Sir James."

James shrugged, refusing to be drawn. "Times have changed, Candelstone. Women have changed. Regardless of what you believe, you will need to deal with Lady Aldrich if you wish to see the letter. We will expect you at ten tomorrow morning. I have nothing more to say." He turned away from Candelstone to signal the waiter for another coffee, the one before him having grown cold.

Lord Candelstone stood there a moment more, a thunderous expression in his eyes. Then he compressed his lips tightly, a frown pulling his eyebrows together. He turned on his heel to leave.

Soothcoor whistled softly between his teeth. "You have set the dog on the fox. Best beware the fox doesn't kill the dog."

James leaned back in his chair. "Little chance of that," he said dismissively.

"Do you have any idea what this matter of national security might be?"

James shook his head. "No. The magistrate in Folkestone believes it is the smuggling activity that picked up after they sent Napoleon to Elba. Even though Napoleon is in France again, it hasn't curbed the free runners."

"Hmm."

The waiter came up with his coffee refill.

"Soothcoor, do you know Kate Sinclair?" James asked after the waiter left.

"The actress?"

"Yes. I understand she used to be under Lord Aldrich's protection," James said.

Soothcoor nodded. "I seem to recall that from a year ago, but for the past nine months, she's been the *chère amie* of Viscount Farnol. She has a snug little cottage in St. Giles. Why do you ask?"

"The letter Lord Aldrich sent to his wife tells her to contact Kate Sinclair," James said over the rim of his coffee cup.

"Contact his former mistress?" Soothcoor asked.

"Yes. Odd, isn't it? She must know a piece of the puzzle. I think my wife and Lady Aldrich would enjoy a night at the theater tonight. Would your box be available, or have you bequeathed it to someone else?"

"Nay, 'tis available, though I have heard that some young bucks have taken to assuming it for themselves. 'Bout time they learned 'tis not for their use."

"Would you care to join us?"

"Aye, might be entertaining."

"Then I will take my leave of you until then. I have much to do before we meet."

8

The play had just begun and the Earl of Soothcoor was before them in the theater box. He smiled as they entered. It split his long face in half.

"Soothcoor, I don't ever think I've seen you smile unless in sardonic amusement," James said. Soothcoor was known for his dour expression and temperament. Only a few of his close friends knew of his kind heart and enthusiasm for helping others.

"Aah, I try to be pleasant fer the ladies, and you are not appreciative. Lady Branstoke, it is a pleasure to see you again," he said, taking her hand and lifting it to his lips.

"And you as well, my lord. Please, let me make you known to my friend, Lady Aldrich. Elinor, this is the Earl of Soothcoor, an old friend of James' as you can tell by the banter."

"My lord," Elinor said shyly, dipping a slight curtsy. Still new to her position in life as the wife of a baron, Elinor was not comfortable around titled aristocracy.

"My lady. Allow me to show you to a seat by me," Lord Soothcoor said.

She nodded and allowed him to help her with her things as she took a seat.

"I have known your husband since he completed his studies and came to London—umm, probably ten years ago," he told her.

She looked at him. "I'm sorry, my lord. I am not sure how to take that comment. I am aware of my husband's reputation before our marriage. Some people say such things in kindness, others in criticism."

He placed his long-fingered hand on hers. "My dear, I say it with kindness. Lord Aldrich was an enjoyable companion for an evening's entertainment. I would say I am the one people may observe with criticism as I do not have the lightness of manner that has blessed your husband."

She smiled at him. "Thank you for that. Will you point out Miss Sinclair when she is on stage?" Elinor asked him.

"Yes. She is not a starring actress, hers is a minor, though comic role in this play," he said. "I find her quite talented in the comic roles."

"Unlike Mrs. Siddons."

He nodded. "The dramas and the dramatic actresses are favored."

"Which is why, financially, she has to have a protector," Cecilia said from the other side of Elinor.

"That is a sad commentary on women in our society, is it not? That she cannot make enough money as an actress to live independently, but needs a protector? At least it is understood by many men—though sadly not all—that when they part ways, the woman receives compensation in some way for her future."

Elinor and Cecilia looked at him in surprise. James laughed. "You have discovered the hidden depth to our dour friend. When we are next in London, you should ask him to introduce you to his charities."

Soothcoor frowned at James. "But tonight we are here to assist Lady Aldrich," he said, steering the conversation in another direction.

"Do you know who Miss Sinclair's current protector is?" Elinor asked.

"Viscount Farnol," Soothcoor said.

Cecilia frowned. "I do not know that gentleman," she said.

James leaned forward. "He is in the fourth box from the stage, on the second level. You can see him with a bunch of other gentlemen. The tall, very thin man with high collar points. He towers over the others."

Soothcoor snorted. "I kicked out Timmy Wainbottom and Jerry Jessup from freeloading in me box before you came. They are with Farnol now."

Cecilia tilted her head. "He looks quite serious."

"He has a more serious demeanor. I would wager they were not invited to join him," James drawled.

"There, the woman dressed as the housekeeper, with the outrageous oversized headdress, that is your Miss Sinclair."

"Oh, gracious, she is tall, too. She must have towered over Simon," Elinor said.

"I don't think that matters when one is in a horizontal position," Cecilia whispered behind her fan to Elinor.

Elinor colored. "No, I suppose not," her voice squeaked.

Cecilia laughed. "I am very bad, I know."

"No, no, not at all," she assured her friend, smiling. She looked back across the theater. –No!" she screamed. She rose from her chair and pointed into the audience. "No!"

A man fired a gun toward the stage. Miss Sinclair stumbled, falling backward on the floor. Screaming came from every corner of the theater.

"Stay here!" James ordered as he ran out of the box, Soothcoor behind him.

Cecilia and Elinor leaned over the edge of the box. "I think I see her moving," Cecilia said, trying to peer between the surrounding people. Someone closed the red stage curtain, catching some thespians in its path. They fought against the enveloping folds to get behind the curtain.

"Did you get a good look at the man who fired the gun?" Cecilia asked Elinor.

"No, no. I just saw this gun and, and—" She started to cry.

"It's okay," Cecilia said. She put her arm around her and guided her back to her seat.

"What's happening?" she wailed. "First Simon, now his former mistress..."

"The incidents may not be related," Cecilia said helplessly.

"You don't believe that," Elinor declared.

Cecilia sighed and looked out at the theater uproar. "You are right, I don't."

"I can't just sit here," Elinor said agitatedly. "We must find out what is happening. We must find out if she is all right!"

"I agree. Grab your things," Cecilia said.

"You are not going to argue with me?" Elinor asked as she gathered up her belongings.

"No, for I am of the same mind, but I didn't wish to leave you alone."

They left the box to the wide, carpeted gallery

that provided access to the boxes. Other people were in the gallery as well, talking in hushed accents with one another, wondering what happened, what to do.

Cecilia led Elinor to the far stairway. More people thronged that area. They grabbed each other's hands so they wouldn't get separated. Elinor, as the taller of the two, moved in front of Cecilia and pushed and prodded a path for them toward the backstage entrance.

"I see the earl!" Elinor said, glancing back at Cecilia as they wormed their way between the people milling about. She led Cecilia in that direction.

"Sometimes I really detest being short," Cecilia complained.

"You are not short, you are petite," Elinor countered.

"Humph."

"Soothcoor! My lord!" Elinor cried out.

He turned at her voice. A sharp frown carved into his tall brow. "And what might you ladies be doing down here?" he asked.

"We couldn't just sit up there, not knowing anything," Cecilia said.

A man jostled her in passing and she almost pitched forward. Soothcoor reached out to steady her. "Easy, lass. This is why you shouldna be here. 'Tis craziness!"

"Where's James?" Cecilia asked.

"With Miss Sinclair and Viscount Farnol in the theater office."

"Is she okay?" asked Elinor.

Soothcoor turned toward her. "Yes. The bullet caught that monstrous wig and hat she wore."

"I'd like to see her," Elinor said.

"Nay, my lady," demurred Soothcoor gently. "That be not the best idea."

She glared at him. "Nevertheless, I will see her. Aldrich cared for her once. I owe her that," Elinor declared stoutly as she looked about the crowd.

Cecilia nodded. "I agree with her, my lord. Is it this way?" she asked, heading forward. There was a press of cast members and young dandies near an open door. Cecilia wove her way through the people, murmuring apologies as she went, Elinor following.

Soothcoor threw up his hands and trailed behind, muttering about the contrariness of women.

Viscount Farnol was trying to close the office door, but Cecilia and Elinor slipped under his arm.

"Out!" Farnol yelled, turning to open the door again, to push them out the door. James pushed against the door to keep it closed.

"This is my wife, Lady Branstoke, and Lady Aldrich."

"Lady Aldrich?" Kate Sinclair exclaimed.

The office was small, with a slant-top desk with shelves above at one end. Miss Sinclair sat in the chair in front of the desk, the remains of her elaborate headdress in her lap. She started to get up.

"Please, stay in your seat," Cecilia said. "You have had a terrible fright." She looked at her husband. "James, do we know who shot at Miss Sinclair? Was she clearly the intended victim?"

"We can't say for sure," James said. "However, she was at least ten steps away from any of the other cast members when the shot was fired."

"What's your interest in this? What's going on?" Farnol demanded.

"It might have something to do with my husband," Lady Aldrich said quietly.

"You are Lord Aldrich's wife?" Kate Sinclair asked.

"Yes. He wrote me a letter that makes no sense. We fear it might be some sort of code. You are mentioned in the letter with an instruction for me to come see you."

Farnol scowled down at Miss Sinclair. "I thought you were done with Aldrich," he said. "If I thought—"

"I am done with Aldrich, as I told you. I have not lied, David," Miss Sinclair said.

Farnol frowned suspiciously at her.

"Easy, my lord. We believe what she says is true," James said. "But there may be information she can give us from before they parted that can be of some assistance to us."

"What do you mean *assistance*?" blustered Farnol.

"My husband has been missing for almost four weeks now," Elinor said quietly. "He might be dead."

"What?" Miss Sinclair cried out.

"There was a carriage accident, and they found his portmanteau in the wreckage, but there was no sign of Simon, nor any blood, other bodies, nor horses. Nothing like that. It looked staged. We don't understand why," Elinor said, her eyes brimming with unshed tears.

"You poor thing," Miss Sinclair said, reaching out a hand toward her.

"I have a letter from him that is very strange," Elinor continued, stepping closer to Miss Sinclair. "His valet couldn't understand the allusions in the letter, except for your name. Would you read it please, and see what you may make of the letter?"

"Yes, of course!" Miss Sinclair said, straightening up in her chair. She held her hand out.

There was a pounding on the office door. "This is the stage manager; let me in my office!"

James and Farnol ignored him. Elinor took the letter out of her reticule with shaking fingers and passed it to Kate Sinclair.

Miss Sinclair skimmed the letter, her brow furrowing. She started shaking her head even before she'd finished. "I'm afraid I do not know what this letter is about. Baby names?" She looked up at Elinor.

"No, I'm not breeding," Elinor said.

"Could that be a way to refer to his associates?" Cecilia asked, looking up at her husband.

James nodded. "Possibly. Miss Sinclair, can you give us the names of gentlemen he associated with?"

"Yes! And one of those men is why I quit the relationship."

"You quit the relationship?"

"I know that is hard to believe, a woman of my career and place in life leaving a protector, but so it was. And I knew Lord Farnol was interested, so it didn't seem so great a risk," she said, looking up at the viscount.

He relaxed a little and raised his chin. "Well, that was well done of you, Kate. Very well done."

"I like to think so," she said, smiling up at him.

"But can you give us names?" James persisted.

"A few. There was Lord Wheaten."

"I have met Lord Wheaten," Elinor said.

Kate smiled. "He was an odd little man, always talking about the rich having too much and how we needed to give to the poor. —A Captain Dunnett, who I gathered is typically stationed in Dover. I did not care for him much, a bit too full of himself. There was a man Simon just called Oakes. He didn't introduce us. He was kind of a rough-looking sort. Quite without gentlemanly refinement to my mind. He was constantly toadying Lord Wheaten."

The stage manager resumed pounding on the door. "I'll have this door broken down if you don't let me in!"

"In a moment, you shall have your office back," James yelled back.

"Now see, laddie, I told you not to fratch yurself. Lord Branstoke will give you yur office back," they heard Soothcoor humoring the man.

"What are they doing in there? What is going on? I have a theater to run. This is a disaster! Kate Sinclair, you are fired! Do you hear me, fired!"

"Oh, no! No!" Kate rose from her chair. "I've got to, I've got to—"

"Wait! Are those all the men? Which one did you object to?"

"No, none of those three. The man that I warned Lord Aldrich away from was Bishop Yarnell."

"Who's Bishop Yarnell?" Cecilia asked as the door shuddered, then ripped from its hinges into the room.

9

"Who is Bishop Yarnell?" Cecilia asked again when they were in their carriage heading back to their townhouse.

When the young bucks who enthusiastically broke down the door for the theater manager, burst into the room, there were cheers, laughter, and—from some who thought they'd burst in on an orgy—cries of dismay. The theater manager pushed the men aside, yelling at everyone to leave. In the hall before the office, there were cries of, "What's going on?" and, "Is there blood?"

Kate Sinclair waved the damaged headdress at the theater manager. "Look at this! Look at this! He nearly killed me! Did you catch him?"

"No, ah—"

"No? No? Oh, I feel faint. Farnol!" she cried as she fainted toward the viscount.

Manfully, he caught her. Cecilia and James exchanged amused glances at her theatrics.

James used the additional confusion to extricate the three of them from the room, and soon they were outside awaiting their carriage. James promised to update Soothcoor on the morrow, and soon they were away from the theater.

"Yarnell is not a name Simon has mentioned," Elinor offered.

"Yarnell owns a gaming hell on South Audley Street, but that is not why Miss Sinclair holds him in derision. Forgive my plain speaking; however, to put the matter in context, he is also known to play rough in the bedroom."

"Oh, no!" Elinor and Cecilia cried simultaneously.

"There have been rumors of serious injuries," he said, compressing his lips tightly. "By the way, did you get the letter from Simon back from her?"

"No! I quite forgot!" Elinor exclaimed. She clapped a hand to her cheek. "How could I have been so remiss?"

James drily laughed. "How could you not! It was pandemonium in there. But that puts us in a bad place for our meeting with Candelstone tomorrow."

"No, not at all. That was only a copy," Cecilia said. "Elinor and I made copies before you returned home from your club."

He nodded. "I meant to request you do that exercise. I am pleased and relieved to know you did." He looked out the carriage window, then turned his head to look up at the dark night sky as they turned down their street. "It has started to rain. The groom will ring the bell to summon a footman with an umbrella."

"I'M NERVOUS," Elinor admitted the next morning as they gathered in the gold parlor on the ground floor to await Lord Candelstone. She had pulled the tambour frame she had insisted on bringing to the city, up to where she sat on a small gold and brown striped damask sofa, but had so far only restlessly picked through her skeins of thread.

"Why?" James asked.

"I don't know," she said. She placed a hand against her stomach. "I just have this churning here that won't subside."

"I saw you hardly ate anything at breakfast," Cecilia said.

"Nerves, I suppose. I can't stop thinking about someone shooting at Miss Sinclair! And I don't know the Candelstones well, though they did introduce me to Simon. I especially don't know Lord Candelstone."

"Yes, Candelstone mentioned something to the effect of introducing you yesterday when I saw him at my club," James said. "How did that come about? How do they know you?"

"Through my father. My father had dealings with Lord Candelstone early last year." She paused. "I'm not telling this in the proper order. Let me start again."

"Take your time," James said.

"I told you my father deals in wool and wool cloth."

"Yes, I remember," James said.

Cecilia nodded.

"Many people believe that the finest, softest wool is loomed outside of England, that it is beyond our English mills' capability. My father has been working to change that perception; however, not all have been pleased with his efforts.

"Lord Candelstone heard rumors about a plan to burn down the England manufactories, to ensure England is forced to buy their finished cloth from other countries."

"A rather radical form of balance of trade," James said drily.

"I suppose," Elinor said. "Anyway, my father's mill was among the businesses targeted. Lord Candelstone appealed to my father's loyalty to the crown to persuade him to allow Candelstone to use his mill as bait for the arsonists. He promised no harm would come because of his assistance."

"But that did not prove to be the case," James concluded.

"No, sadly, it did not. Not only did my father lose one of his mills, but a woman and her son were badly burned escaping."

"Oh, no!" Cecilia exclaimed. "What happened to them?"

"Sadly, the boy lost the use of the fingers on one hand from beating out the flames on his mother. His mother lives with scars on her face and chest."

"How old was the boy?" Cecilia asked.

"Thirteen, I believe. Because of the egregious nature of their injuries, they can no longer work. Father provided them with a cottage, a plot of land, and a pension for life. Along with ongoing medical care. I understand the pulling on the scars can be quite painful."

"How awful!" Cecilia said. "But what does this have to do with you meeting Lord Aldrich?"

"Father was furious," Elinor explained. "Yes, insurance covered the mill, but it didn't cover lost productivity, nor the relief for that poor woman and her son. He threatened to take the story to *The Times*. Lord Candelstone asked what he could do to help repay for the loss. Father rather sarcastically said he could see that I was married into society. And without blinking an eye, Lord Candelstone agreed! He said he had just the gentleman in mind. A charming fellow, a little spendthrift and in need of a wife with funds, but a good sort."

"Lord Aldrich," James said.

"Yes, Lord Simon Aldrich. Lady Candelstone, who is a lovely woman, took me under her wing and saw that I was dressed appropriately, knew the popular dances—even the waltz—and learned the nuances of society." She smiled to herself at her memories. "The Candelstones then introduced me to Simon at a soiree at their Belgrave Square mansion."

"When was this?" James asked.

"At the end of last year's spring London season. We both knew the purpose of the introduction." She straightened and pushed her hands down into the folds on her gray gown on her lap. "I was so frightened, but it struck me how handsome Simon was, and how terribly, terribly gentle he acted toward me." She sighed and a smile lit a glow in her eyes. "I think I fell a little in love with him at that first meeting." Her smile faded as she looked from one to the other. "Silly, I know, a wool merchant's daughter mooning for a baron."

"Nonsense," Cecilia said. "You are a woman, he is a man, that is enough."

Elinor laughed slightly at Cecilia's pronouncement, then continued with her story. "We didn't see each other over the summer. I was forlorn and thought I had given him a distaste for me. I later learned he was at Bartlett Hall, working with his tenants who, he admitted to me, he had forsaken for too long. We didn't meet again until after Michaelmas when he returned to London. He told me he thought of me a great deal and he asked if he may request an audience with my father. I was shocked but delighted.

No, we didn't know each other well; however, we were comfortable in each other's company and we both were looking to wed, and so we were in November."

Cecilia smiled mistily. "Thank you for sharing your story with us," she said.

"Owing to your previous acquaintance with Lord Candelstone, you know he may request to speak with you in private," James warned.

"Yes, I understand that, but honestly, I do not think I would like to do so. I do like Lady Candelstone; however, her husband made me feel uncomfortable, as he was always watching me. Like he searched, looking for something in my person to condemn. He was always circumspect, but distant. I was a nuisance he had to deal with. Another tool for him to shape and use."

Sir James nodded. "As we told Melville, we know a gentleman who worked for Candelstone. His summation of Candelstone wasn't as a sympathetic gentleman for any needs save his own. King and Country first before everything—family, health, wealth. Everything."

"James," Cecilia said thoughtfully. "Do you suppose Lord Aldrich worked for Lord Candelstone?"

"Aldrich? I wouldn't have thought so, but now that you say that, I suppose we can't rule that out."

"What makes you suggest that, Cecilia?" Elinor asked.

"Because from what I have heard, it doesn't sound as if Lord Candelstone does anything without a reason. He had a reason for assisting your father, to keep him mum on the circumstances of the fire, but why Aldrich?"

"That is an interesting observation, my dear. Very interesting. I remember Havelock telling me how Candelstone encouraged feigned behavior."

"Exactly, and as a user of feigned behavior, it is something I can comprehend," Cecilia returned wryly.

James laughed.

There was a knock on the parlor door. "Excuse me, Sir James, but you have a visitor below. Lord Candelstone, baronet."

"Thank you, Charwood." He rose to his feet. "Please escort his lordship up here and bring the tea and coffee service."

"Immediately," Charwood said, bowing his way out of the room.

James motioned Elinor to change seats to the one he'd vacated. He helped her move her tambour frame. He did not want Candelstone to sit beside her. That might prove too difficult for the woman to resist his persistence and blandishments.

Cecilia picked up the sewing she had been working on, attaching a length of lace edging to a new handkerchief.

"Lord Candelstone," Charwood announced in stentorian accents a moment later.

James straightened from his lounge against the fireplace and walked toward Candelstone to grasp the man's arm.

"Well met, Lord Candelstone."

"Sir James," he said differentially, then turned to bow to Cecilia and Elinor. "Lady Branstoke, Lady Aldrich."

The ladies inclined their heads and murmured greetings.

He turned back to Lady Aldrich. "I am so sorry we have to meet again under these circumstances," he said. "You were hardly married, hardly had time to get to know one another, and he is gone."

She smiled slightly. "Thank you for your condolences."

"Of course, of course! Lady Candelstone and I introduced you, so we feel a modicum of responsibility for his life and death."

"Why would you feel responsible for him?" James asked.

He rocked back on his heels. "In relation to her ladyship, of course, as we introduced them," he said bluffly.

"Yes, we heard that. Please have a seat," James said, gesturing him to a chair away from Elinor. "How did that introduction come about, if I might ask? I have never imagined you as a matchmaker, Candelstone," James said.

Candelstone laughed. He lifted the tails of his coat and sat down. "Yes, I can see that. I hardly countenance it myself. All happenstances, you know," he said airily. "I felt the nation owed Mr. Edgerton as one of his mills burned down due to an unfortunate mistake an associate of mine made while on government business."

"You felt you owed him," James repeated flatly.

Elinor shot a glance up at Sir James, a slight frown on her lips.

"Yes, sad affair. Radicals, you know."

"No, I'm afraid I don't," James said. "What do you mean?"

Candelstone laughed. "You know I cannot tell you details, home office secrets and all that."

"Yes, you are in the midst of the spy business." James crossed his legs and leaned back in his chair, his posture that of ease and boredom.

Candelstone frowned at James' attitude. "Napoleon has necessitated these unsavory tasks. We must fight like with like. England is overrun with his spies. We *must* keep them in check," he finished forcefully.

Cecilia and James exchanged quick glances. Lord Candelstone was as much a fanatic as any fanatic he chased.

"Was Lord Aldrich one of your spies?" James asked.

"What? Eh, why would you ask that? No, no, of course not! Genial fellow, not the sort for secrets, if you know what I mean." His eyes darted between them. He brought his handkerchief up to blot his upper lip, then returned it to his pocket.

Cecilia thought his protest overly strong, but returned her eyes to her careful stitching.

A knock on the door was followed by Charwood entering with tea and coffee. Cecilia set her handwork aside and rose to pour the beverages.

"So, how did you come to arrange for Lord Aldrich to meet Lady Aldrich?" she asked as she poured him a cup of tea. "Milk or sugar?"

"Just milk, please."

She added milk and then handed him the cup. "What was your motivation for the introduction?"

"Well, Lady Branstoke, if you must know, it was all Lady Candelstone. She is quite the romantic," he said with a slightly forced laugh. "As we have not been blessed with our own children, she has endeavored to take under wing various young people. She took a liking to Lord Aldrich. Always pleasant address, good in company, and when you needed another gentleman at the table, he could be counted on, you know, that sort of thing. Never offends. Might play a little too deep at times, but all young bucks do that when amongst their fellows."

"Sounds like the résumé for a spy," James observed.

Candelstone laughed heartily. He pulled out his kerchief from his pocket again and this time dabbed at his brow.

"If Lord Aldrich was not one of your spies," Cecilia said pensively, her eyes wide open and quite guileless, "then why send Captain Melville for his correspondence? And why ask for his letter to Lady Aldrich?"

"Oh, well, you see, Lady Branstoke, Lord Aldrich had written to me. Yes. He wrote to me." He took a sip of his tea. "He knew my interest in keeping Napoleon at bay and now that the damned Corsican—excuse my language, my ladies—now that Napoleon has escaped Elba, he knew we are all attentive to any communications, any whispers as to his plans."

Candelstone forced a hearty laugh again. "Well, Aldrich fancied himself working for the foreign office. Offered his services once. We turned him down, of course, too frippery a fellow. But recently, he thought he'd come upon something important."

"Lord Candelstone," James said with a touch of exasperation at the truth-distortions he suspected, "that is all interesting, but how does that explain your interest in the letter Aldrich sent his wife, and to such an extent that Captain Melville endeavored to steal it from her? He actually snatched it from my wife's hand! He insisted the letter is a matter of national importance, as you did yourself yesterday afternoon. When Melville informed you I was coming to London, you set an urchin to watch my townhouse and to follow me to inform you where I went. Why would you do that?"

"What!" Candelstone shifted in his chair. "No, I never. You are jumping to conclusions."

"That won't service, Candelstone," James said severely. "The people who work for you are better actors than you are. When you came to White's, you were looking for me and when we finished speaking, you immediately left. What do you believe is in that letter that you so strongly want to see? And does it have anything to do with someone attempting to kill Miss Sinclair at the theater last night?"

"You have heard of that already," Candelstone said flatly.

"We were there as Miss Sinclair is mentioned in Aldrich's letter to his wife and so we wished to speak to Miss Sinclair after the play."

Candelstone drew in a deep breath, then let it out. His lips compressed and released several times as he considered his response.

"I'm sure you know Lord Jasper Wheaten," he said finally.

"Yes."

"He is forever protesting the war subsidies England sends to our allies, subsidies that are important if we are to keep the French at bay. When Napoleon was sent to Elba, we still had promised another payment to our allies. Lord Wheaten was furious that we would still pay for friendship. Bribing others to align with us, he calls it. He said those funds should go to the veterans returned from war. He does not understand foreign policy and political diplomacy."

"He has a great interest in our soldiers," Elinor said. "A humanitarian interest."

Candelstone nodded. "There was debate at the highest ranks of government whether this year's payments should be made, but then Napoleon escaped and the matter was no longer in question. We need our allies' assistance. They have faced more of the war effects than we have, in their own countries with the depravations Napoleon and his troops did. Their coffers have been drained. We need to bolster their continued efforts, give them a backbone to stand with us until we can once and for all get rid of Napoleon."

"So, from this we are to infer that Lord Wheaten is planning to steal the subsidies?" Cecilia asked.

"Not planning, your ladyship. He has already done so."

10

"Stolen? How much are we talking about?" James asked. "I read in *The Times* that our last year's spend was estimated at ten million pounds."

"Not the whole of the national budget for subsidies," tempered Candelstone. "No, no, nothing like that. More like one million pounds."

"That is still a sum to take my breath away," said Cecilia.

"How is my husband involved with this?" Elinor asked crisply.

"He alerted me to the plan," Candelstone said.

"So how is it, then, that the theft occurred?" Elinor asked. "Why didn't you stop it?"

"The theft could not be done by one man, particularly not a man of Lord Wheaten's health," explained Candelstone.

"Health ailments can be manufactured." Cecilia said, glancing over at her husband. He responded with a sly wink and a smile to her.

"True, Lady Branstoke; however, in this case, the size of the subsidies shipment would have required more than one man, several sturdy wagons, and strong horses. In addition, some boxes were quite large as not all the subsidy payment was made in specie. This time much was in armament; the latest and best weapons English manufacturers can provide."

Elinor cocked her head to the side as she looked up at him, her brow wrinkling in confusion. "Again, I'll ask. Why didn't you stop it?"

"My dear Lady Aldrich," he condescended, "we want all the thieves captured. Wheaten has been recruiting for like-minded compatriots for six months. Unfortunately, it appears Wheaten has more hair than wit. Some of his band of thieves have questionable motives."

"Such as Bishop Yarnell," James stated.

Candelstone nodded. "Yes. We were concerned when Aldrich indicated Wheaten was impressed with Yarnell's enthusiasm for the plot. Yarnell convinced Wheaten he was as upset as Wheaten was at the use of the subsidies and strongly said they needed to go to our veterans. Because we don't trust Yarnell, and believe he was playing Wheaten, we asked Aldrich to stay a part of the band of thieves."

"Yes, I should think you would not trust Yarnell. He runs a gaming hall that has a questionable reputation for honest play," James said. He couldn't understand what Candelstone hoped to gain by allowing Yarnell to continue to play Wheaten. There was a pattern emerging he did not like.

"So why did someone shoot at Miss Sinclair?" Cecilia asked.

"We believe she was, and is, a target because she knows the men involved in the plot, though she may not realize that. She knows the names of some of the men who were buzzing around Wheaten, as Aldrich was one of those and she was with him. We think someone may have realized this and wanted to ensure she couldn't tell any tales," Candelstone explained.

"None of this sounds like the Lord Wheaten I met," Elinor said.

"I understand, Lady Aldrich," Candelstone patronized. "We don't believe Wheaten is interested in the weapons, only the gold. Truthfully, he may not have been aware of the weapons at the time of the robbery as the decision to send weapons was made shortly before the subsidies were gathered."

"Have you talked to Miss Sinclair?" James asked.

Candelstone sighed and regretfully shook his head. "No, Viscount Farnol is not allowing any visitors at the present. I'm trying to see if he will allow a woman to visit so we can get to her that way. I was hoping the letter might have provided an indication; however, Melville says it didn't, only that Miss Sinclair might know names."

"She does," Cecilia said.

"How do you know this?"

"She told us, last evening after the attempt on her life," Cecilia said.

"She gave us four names," James continued. "Two you are already familiar with: Lord Wheaten and Bishop Yarnell. The other two she named were Captain Dunnett, who she thought was stationed out of Dover, and Oakes, a name I'm not familiar with."

"Captain Dunnett!" Candelstone exclaimed. He threw his hands up as he stood. "This is disastrous! I must get back to the home office and warn them." He paced their parlor. "He's been party to all of our communiques. No wonder we can't find the subsidies. He knows we are hunting, and he has gone to ground with them!"

"Elinor, before Lord Candelstone leaves, I think you should show him the letter," James said.

She compressed her lips tightly as she frowned, but she relented. "All right." She leaned over to pick her embroidery basket off the floor and shift skeins of thread aside to bring out the letter. "Here." She extended her hand, then drew it back when he would have taken the letter. "You will not grab it and try to run away, will you, as your Captain Melville attempted to do?"

"My dear lady, I am past the age of running anywhere."

She handed the letter to him.

Lord Candelstone sat down again and pulled a pair of glasses out of his waistcoat pocket and put them on. "Damned nuisance these things, but I can't read a thing without them." He unfolded the letter and read it aloud.

It is late and I am more tired than usual. I conclude it is too much salt sea air.

"This confirms he is near the coast. Good."

But I must answer your letter before I sleep. Your questions prey upon my mind.

No. Do not go to Margate. I was there—briefly last June, before spending 8 days at Penwick Park.

Candelstone looked up. "He is trying to relay something here, but I don't know what. I believe he is saying he is not in Margate. But the June, and the eight days at Penwick Park, I don't understand. Penwick Park is the estate of Mr. and Mrs. Litton. They are out of the country at the Congress of Vienna, but Miss Jane Grantley and her aunt are staying there with the Litton children. Beautiful estate, rolling hills, has a folly with a telescope on the property. Penwick Park must be a stand-in for someplace else. I'll get my people thinking on this." He looked down at the letter again.

It was a rackety place. Entirely unsuitable for a woman in your condition. And before you ask, I shall say the same for Brighton. Choose some place between the two in distance.

"Ah, he is saying he is someplace between Margate and Brighton. That is a large area! Not much help there."

If the weather turns sultry and too unbearable before I return, ask your folks to go with you. The chalk cliffs are lovely, but be careful you don't turn an ankle walking on the stones.

I have no suggestions for baby names. Ask Kate. She's always interested in familial connections. It was she who suggested Simon.

"And we know Miss Kate Sinclair had the names. How did you know *Kate* referred to Miss Sinclair?"

"Through my husband's valet, Mr. Cavanaugh. That was the only Kate he could think of," Elinor said.

"Candelstone, don't you find his use of the word *folks* to be odd? Elinor's mother is deceased, so why would he say *folks*? Might have he been referring to Folkestone?" Cecilia suggested.

"Excellent! Lady Branstoke, I do believe you are correct. And aren't the chalk cliffs where a carriage with his portmanteau was found? He is getting closer with his directions."

Regrettably, I cannot recommend a military career for your cousin. He is not officer material. If he insists, he'll have to look elsewhere for his commission money. The Iron Duke will do better without officers of his ilk.

"I think here he is telling us there is a military man involved, who we now know to be Captain Dunnett," Candelstone said.

Finally, turn to Mr. Ash on all estate matters. I am aware Mr. Miller feels in command. Such is not the case. When in doubt, you may consult your father.

"Are Ash and Miller people in your employ, Lady Aldrich?"

"No! Neither."

"Then I think he is using *Miller* for Lord Wheaten and he is telling us Lord Wheaten is not in control."

"Perhaps by *Mr. Ash* he is referring to the Mr. Oakes Miss Sinclair mentioned?" suggested Sir James.

"Possibly, whoever that may be," Candelstone said. *Your obedient servant,*

Simon

"Interesting how he signs off as well. *Your obedient servant.* Did he call himself that to you, Lady Aldrich?"

"No, not at all," she responded austerely. Cecilia looked at her quizzically.

"Then we can assume he was trying to relay another message that we don't understand. I shall need to think on this," Candelstone said, nodding to himself.

Elinor set her tambour frame aside and rose to her feet. "I, on the other hand, do not need to think further. What I conclude is my husband is in trouble and you have allowed this to happen just as you allowed my father's mill to be destroyed by waiting and not acting on information you had. You undoubtedly had to think on it!"

"Lady Aldrich!" protested Lord Candelstone. "I hardly think—"

"I'm not surprised," Elinor said repressively.

Cecilia laughed, and Sir James looked down at his shoes to hide his smile. *The pattern emerges.*

Elinor snatched the letter from Lord Candelstone's hand, then went to the bellpull to summon the butler.

"Lady Aldrich, if I might keep that letter? I understand how upsetting this may be for you. I am not an unfeeling gentleman."

"Ha! I disagree. Remember, I was in your home many times last spring with Lady Candelstone. I have your measure."

The door to the parlor opened to admit Charwood. He looked at Sir James.

"I believe Lady Aldrich has decided it is time for Lord Candelstone to leave. Please escort our guest out," James said.

"At once," Charwood said, standing aside for Lord Candelstone to pass. "My lord?"

"Young woman, you have no understanding of the importance of the politics involved. But given your antecedents, perhaps that is understandable."

Cecilia gasped in outrage. "How dare you! *Out!*" she said, rising to her feet and pointing to the door.

Candelstone looked with surprise in Cecilia's direction. Then he turned, scowling at James.

"Sir James, I shall see you at White's later," Candelstone said huffily before stalking past the butler.

When the door had closed after him, Elinor returned to her seat on the sofa. "Thank you for supporting me in having Lord Candelstone leave. I realized as soon as I rang the bellpull, I was being presumptuous."

"You were not presumptuous. You acted correctly. It was that man who did not!" exclaimed Cecilia. "The absolute effrontery of that man is beyond all."

"I think you are correct, Elinor," James said. "Lord Candelstone likes to have events play out."

"He's like a spider watching others get caught in his web," observed Cecilia as she sat down again.

"Precisely. A good analogy, my love," said James.

"So, James, will you go to your club to see him? That rather sounded like an order, not a request," Cecilia said.

"No. I have no intention of licking Lord Candelstone's boots, or of being pulled into his realm to do his bidding."

"He would likely try to make it sound as if you are the only man for the job and would receive much accolade from the government for your services," Elinor said waspishly.

"Most likely. However, I stand in no need of accolades—except for those from my beautiful wife." He raised her hand to his lips and kissed her knuckles.

"And what should I, pray tell, give your accolades for?" Cecilia asked archly.

He smiled silently down at her. She smiled back.

"Ahem," interrupted Elinor. "This is all edifying, I am certain, but it doesn't clarify what should be our next steps."

James dropped his wife's hand and looked over at her. "I suggest a return to The Seagull."

11

"So, what do you think of Lord Candelstone's story?" Cecilia asked James as the carriage rocked. She and Elinor had taken the forward-facing seat with James across from them, but soon Cecilia moved to sit next to him, removed her bonnet, and rested her head on his shoulder. James wrapped his arm around her. Elinor had fallen asleep, as she had on previous carriage trips. Cecilia envied her that ability. The carriage rocked and bumped too much for her to sleep.

"Plausible, providing subsidies to our allies has been done for hundreds of years. The government tried to make a loan instead of a subsidy to Austria a couple of years ago to make the Whigs happy; however, we have not heard of any repayments to date, nor issued requests for repayments. Usually, Nathan Rothschild handles the subsidies. I have not, however, ever heard of the subsidies being anything other than gold. The weapons are a curious departure."

"If Lord Wheaten stole the subsidies, it would disappoint him that the full amount isn't in gold, he wouldn't have need of weapons. Why should they be missing?" Cecilia asked.

"That's a good question, my dear. I have been considering that as well. I also am drawn back to my visit with Mr. Pollock. One of his footmen looked like a bruiser, the kind that would be beneficial for a smuggler gang."

"Are you thinking Mr. Pollock might be caught up in this?" Cecilia asked.

"I don't know. His estate is called Denwidth Park."

"Hm, quite similar to Penwick Park mentioned in the letter."

"Yes."

"What would be his motivation for being caught up in this theft?" she asked.

"That, I also I don't know," he said pensively. "I believe he is involved with the smugglers, but not with the subsidies theft. The subsidies theft has all the military on heightened alert for irregularities. Might be hard for the smugglers to bring their goods in."

"So perhaps we can use a thief to catch a thief?" Cecilia asked.

"Or at least give us more information than we are likely to gather on our own. These small villages are protective of their own and not likely to take kindly to our asking too many questions."

Cecilia lifted her head from James' shoulder to look up at him. "But how do you approach Mr. Pollock? You can't be sure he is not involved with the subsidies theft."

"Yes, and that is why I'm as yet uncertain how to approach him."

She grimaced, then sighed and laid her head back down. "I'm surprised you are letting Elinor and me come with you, for I know you will be investigating."

"In truth, I would rather you didn't come. However, I know either you, she, or both of you would trail behind no matter what I would say to the contrary, unless I locked you up somewhere."

She gave a little muffled laugh. "You are probably correct."

"I would worry continually about you following. It is better that you are where I can see you!"

"It is the same for me and why I must go with you," she said. "I would worry not knowing what is happening!"

"Then I fear we are a sad couple."

She giggled. "No, I disagree. I think we are the luckiest of couples."

He turned his head and dropped a light kiss on her hair. "Try to rest. We have at least another hour until Summerworth Park."

"I've never been able to sleep in a carriage before, but perhaps with you as my pillow I can."

"ELINOR, stay with us at Summerworth Park tonight," Cecilia heard James say to Elinor.

"Thank you, yours is a kind offer, I know, but I would prefer to return to Bartlett Hall, if for nothing else than to speak with the staff. The events of the last few days have been unsettling for them."

"And for us all," James said.

Cecilia realized she had her head in James' lap and her feet drawn up to the leaf-green velvet seat cushions. She raised her head.

"Ah, awake, she who says she can't sleep in rocking carriages," James said lightly as he helped her to a sitting position.

"I never have slept before. And it was a wondrous little nap. Thank you," she said.

"You are welcome, my lady, and just in time, for we are about to arrive at Bartlett Hall."

"I heard you tell Elinor she should stay with us."

"I did."

She turned toward Elinor. "And I agree with James, Elinor. I know I would feel much better knowing you are with us. There have been too many actions by others that are not understandable. That fact has me concerned."

Elinor smiled at Cecilia. "I am grateful for your concern. It touches my heart to have such good friends. But as I told James, I have an obligation to my staff as well."

"Will you be ready to depart for the coast in the morning?" James asked.

"Yes, and without the retinue, though I wonder if we should take Aisha with us."

"Your lady's maid? Why?" Cecilia asked.

"Because she can go about and ask questions easier than we can. While her sentences may be broken, she is very bright. Sometimes I wonder if she is not just a little lazy with her English," Elinor said ruefully.

"Or, she may feel people speak more freely around her as they assume she does not understand well. That is part of the tactic I use with my feigning ill-health."

"Hmm, yes," Elinor said. "I can imagine that is so."

"If you insist on staying at Bartlett Hall tonight, I will have George Romley, one of my grooms, support your staff to keep watch. Romley was with me during the Peninsular Campaign," James said.

"That is kind of you, but there is no need. My staff can keep watch if you believe there is that need."

"It is no problem, I assure you. And I don't know if

there is a need or not; however, I do not think we
should take the chance," he explained.

Elinor looked down at her hands in her lap, then
looked up at James and smiled slightly. "I honor your
care of me, as I know my husband would. Thank you."

"You are not in this alone, Elinor. You have friends
to support you. We will find out what has happened,"
James said as the carriage drew up before Bartlett
Hall.

Elinor's eyes glistened with unshed tears.

12

"Outta my way! Outta my way! I's gots to see Sar James!" a frantic George Romley bellowed as he pushed past the footman who'd opened the door to his thundering knock.

James was just descending the stairs the next morning, his thoughts on the coming investigation.

"Romley! What are you doing here? You are supposed to be keeping watch at Bartlett Hall."

"Aye, sar," Romley gasped, his sides heaving as he strived to catch his breath. He bent forward, bracing his hands on his bent knees. "I were, but then she done drugged me and the gentry mort piked off!"

"Drugged you? Who drugged you?"

Romley slowly straightened, still struggling with his breath. "That foreign woman, the one from India, they tol' me. She brung me a pint. The ale tasted a mite odd, but I didn't wanna be disrespectful, so I drank it and next I knowed, I couldna keep me peepers open."

James frowned, then took in a deep breath. He hadn't expected this. What the bloody hell was going on?

"Come into the breakfast parlor. You could use some coffee."

"Aye, sar, that I could, thank ye," Romley said.

"Darrel," James said to the dumbfounded footman who lingered in the hall. "Ask Lady Branstoke to join us as soon as possible."

"Yes, sir," the young footman said. He scrambled to run up the stairs.

James watched him and shook his head. "He'll never make butler without a little more decorum," he said ruefully. "But, come, Romley. I promised you some coffee and you could also use some food to clear the last of the drug from your system."

"Thank ye, sar," Romley said as he followed James. Belatedly, he realized he still had his cap on his head. He quickly pulled it off and stuffed it in his waistband.

James poured himself some coffee, then held out the pot to pour some for Romley. His man looked at him with shock, but quickly held out a cup, which James filled before setting the pot down.

"Thank ye, sar," Romley said again, with something akin to awe in his voice. "Might there be any sugar, sar?" he asked tentatively.

"In that bowl, there," James said, indicating an ornate silver sugar bowl with a spoon.

Romley scooped three large teaspoons of sugar into his cup. James surmised he rarely got a chance to have sugar. Perhaps not any sweets at all. For the servants' hall, he would ensure the cook knew to prepare desserts, and the butler would offer sugar and cream for coffee and tea.

"Sit down, Romley."

"Here, sar?" Romley asked, pointing to the seat next to James.

"Yes, here. When Lady Branstoke gets here, you

will tell us the entire story. Afterward, you can check on what horses we have for another trip. You may need to fetch fresh horses from the inn in the village."

"Aye, sar."

"James, Darrel said you wished to see me immediately. –Oh! hello, Mr. Romley," Cecilia said. "I thought you were at Bartlett Hall." She looked quizzically at her husband.

"Best get your tea, my dear," James said. "We have a problem."

Cecilia quickly poured herself a cup of tea and sat down. "What's going on?"

"It appears Elinor's maid drugged Romley last night."

"What?"

Romley nodded. He wiped his mouth on his shirt-sleeve. "And when I woke proper, the mare with the white stockings were gone as were the lady's saddle. I raised a fit and the stable lad said he'd saddled the horse fer the gentry mort and she piked off last night."

"Elinor rode off last night?" Cecilia said, awestruck. "I would not have thought—" Her voice trailed off. "I don't know what to say." She was silent a moment, then turned to look at Romley, her brow furrowing. "Tell us exactly what happened last night from the time you arrived at Bartlett Hall."

"Yes, my lady." He looked from one to the other. "After Sir James asked me to stand watch at Bartlett Hall, I took a lil' nap so's I could stay awake and got to the hall about seven p.m. Everyone was nice enough and seemed concerned for her ladyship. Between her head groom and me, we decided I'd stand first watch, and we would take turns every two hours." He took a sip of his coffee, then ran his tongue over his lips.

"About thirty minutes later, this Indian woman

comes outta the house with a tankard of ale. Tiny thing and very soft speakin'. Said as how she wanted to give me the ale to show she appreciated me bein' there. She chattered at me while I drank their home brew. Tasted odd to me tongue, but not wanting to show disrespect, I finished the ale. Sudden like, I couldna keep me peepers open. I felt real heavy. I knowed they had drugged me but 'tweren't anything I could do about it then."

"Do you know what she gave you?" James asked.

"No, sar."

"Probably laudanum," Cecilia said.

James nodded. "Most likely. At least he should not have lingering ill-effects."

"No." Cecilia looked back at Romley. "So you were asleep," she said. "What time did you wake up?"

"That Indian woman, the one that drugged me, she woke me up."

"She woke you up?" James said as he and Cecilia exchanged quizzical glances.

"Yes, sar. Said I needed to come back here to tell you Lady Aldrich was gone."

Cecilia frowned at James. "First she drugs him so Elinor could ride off, then she wakes him up so he can tell us she's ridden off."

Romley shook his head. "She didna say that, didna say directly she'd piked off. That's wot I larned from the stable lad. She just said as 'ow she were gone."

James leaned back in his chair. "I believe it is time for a conversation with Aisha," he said.

Romely nodded. "Aye, and she'll be expectin' ya, too," he said. He rose from the table to refill his coffee cup as James and Cecilia looked at each other, worried for Elinor's safety.

RATHER THAN IMMEDIATELY DRIVING TO Bartlett Hall, they'd continued with their original plan to prepare for the journey to The Seagull. They would have had to stop by Bartlett Hall to pick up Elinor. Now their visit would be to gather information.

"She must have had some communication from Lord Aldrich," Cecilia said as their traveling carriage drove them to Bartlett Hall.

"That is my thought as well," James said. "I don't believe she would have the courage to strike out on her own."

"Not without knowledge of where she was going," Cecilia returned. "This is all so confusing."

"Yes. What I am still puzzling is Aldrich's role in Candelstone's machinations. I know Candelstone is a rabid fanatic for the crown and believes all means to achieve an end are fair means; however, Aldrich is an odd tool for him to use."

"Unless Aldrich is a skilled player and is not as innocuous as society deems him to be," Cecilia suggested, thinking of her past role in society.

"There is that possibility as well," James said, frowning, as the carriage drew up before the Aldrich manor house.

"Perhaps now, we can put the pieces of the puzzle together," he said as he opened the carriage door. He stepped down, then turned to assist Cecilia. Behind them, they heard the door to the house open.

"You have been so long!" cried out Aisha from the front steps. She hurried down to meet them. This day she wore a charcoal-gray cotton dress instead of her native saree. "Did your man not tell you memsahib gone?"

"Yes, he did," Cecilia said.

"And you and the rest of the staff helped her," James said repressively.

"Yes, yes!" the maid said excitedly.

Cecilia touched her forehead with a gloved hand. "I am confused. Come, let's go inside to discuss the events of last night."

The maid's head bobbled back and forth. "This way, this way," she said, leading them toward the house. At the steps, she gestured they go before her.

Mr. Thomas met them at the door, his face drawn and gray. "Lady Branstoke, Sir James, I am glad you are here. Please come into the parlor."

Mrs. Wembly was before them in the room.

"I didn't know! I swear I didn't know," Mrs. Wembly cried, wringing her hands together. "Oh-oh!" she cried out, tears flowing. She reached for Cecilia's hands.

"Mrs. Wembly, pull yourself together," remonstrated Mr. Thomas. "Your tears and complaints do not help."

"But—" started Mrs. Wembly.

"No, Mrs. Wembly," James said calmly. "Mr. Thomas is correct. We need you to be strong right now."

"Yes, yes, of course," the poor woman said on a hiccup. She dabbed at her eyes with her handkerchief, then held it to her trembling lips.

"Please sit," Cecilia said, turning her toward a chair by the fireplace.

The woman slumped into the chair, her head down, her shoulders shuddering.

Cecilia stared at her a moment, then turned to sit on one of the small sofas. James remained standing by her side.

"Mr. Thomas," James said once Mrs. Wembly was seated and quiet, "what has occurred here? How did Lady Aldrich come to leave Bartlett Hall?"

"It was the letter, sir."

"The letter, what letter? The one that was found in the portmanteau?"

"Yes, sir. Mr. Cavanaugh, he figured out more of the message."

"Where is Cavanaugh?"

"In his room, sir; his gout has been bothering him," the butler said.

James' eyebrow climbed his forehead. "Fetch him here," he said.

"But, sir, he can't walk right now. The pain is bad," Mr. Thomas protested.

"Has he taken any medicine? Has a message been sent to the local doctor to see him?" James asked.

"No, sir, he refused both. Said it would heal better on its own if he just didn't walk."

Mr. Thomas took a slight step backward as James looked thunderingly at him. "If he can refuse medicine and a doctor," James said sternly, "then he is well enough to talk to us. Send a couple of footmen to carry him here."

Mr. Thomas' eyes widened, but he hurried to the parlor door.

"Tommy!" they heard him call out as he closed the door behind him.

"James!" exclaimed Cecilia, surprised at his manner with the butler.

He laid a hand on her shoulder as he looked down at her. "He's hiding, Cecilia. We can't have him hiding when Elinor's life may be at risk," he said softly.

She inhaled deeply, "You are correct." She looked across the room at Mrs. Wembly, huddled in the chair, and at Aisha, standing near her. She frowned. "Aisha, please sit down."

Her head bobbled. "Thank you, memsahib." She sat on the edge of the matching chair to where Mrs. Wembly sat, her posture upright. Only her toes touched the floor. Cecilia noticed that under her English attire, she wore the open-toed sandals of her homeland.

"Aisha," James said. "Mr. Romley said you gave him drugged ale last night."

"Yes, sahib."

"Why did you do that?"

"Memsahib, she say to," she said simply, her dark eyes wide open.

"I see," said James slowly, puzzling how to proceed.

"Memsahib, she miss sahib," she continued, shaking her head at her mistress's sadness. "She so sad. She gets message, she is happy. She go to meet sahib."

"And you woke Mr. Romley in the morning."

"Yes, memsahib say to," she said eagerly. "And to tell him to tell you. Memsahib, she trust you."

"Do you think Elinor intends for us to find her?" Cecilia asked James.

"I don't know, but it sounds like it. We need to talk to Mr. Cavanaugh," he said as they heard a commotion in the hall and Mr. Thomas opened the parlor doors again.

Two footmen had made a chair of their arms where Cavanaugh sat with his arms around their necks.

"Take Mr. Cavanaugh to that sofa," James said, designating a small, dark green sofa edged with gold trim.

Mr. Cavanaugh looked hastily dressed, his hair in

wild disarray. When the men sat him on the sofa, he grimaced as his heel hit the floor.

"Lad, can you help me get my foot up?" he said to the footman as that worthy turned to leave.

"Yes, sir," he said. Gently, he lifted Mr. Cavanaugh's foot and set it on the edge of the sofa. "Will that do, sir?" the footman asked.

"I guess it will have to," the valet said in a quarrelsome, unthankful tone.

Once the man was settled, James stood in front of the sofa, looking down at him. "Mr. Cavanaugh, Mr. Thomas tells me you figured out more of the message in the letter."

"Yes."

James stared at him, waiting. He would not give the man sympathy, nor was he allowing him to be disrespectful. Something had happened in the last few days that had turned this man from wanting to help to querulous and discourteous. Finding out what that was could be as important as discovering his thoughts on the letter.

"Yes, Sir James," he finally amended.

"Come, do not make me pry it out of you," James said. "Lady Aldrich could be in danger."

"Well, she should have taken me with her, like I told her last night!" Cavanaugh flashed back at him.

Mrs. Wembly wailed again at his outburst. Cecilia and James frowned at her. Aisha stood up and crossed to Mrs. Wembly's side, laying a comforting hand on her shoulder.

James looked back at the valet. "Why should she have taken you with her?"

"Because of the money, of course. Never would have thought Lord Aldrich to be a party to theft, but that Lord Wheaten's valet had the right of it."

"You are referring to the foreign subsidies theft."

"Yes. That man was all giddy about it. Could hardly contain himself and let it slip that he and Lord Wheaten were going to steal it. For the poor veterans, he said. Ha. I thought it all a hum, Lord Wheaten being so old. And I never thought Lord Aldrich knew about it or would be party to it. Just goes to show you don't know people when you think you do. I'd a taken him more for a King and Country man. It's no wonder that the bastard wouldn't take me with him when he left three days after Lord Wheaten's visit."

"So, what in that letter led you to believe Lord Aldrich was involved in the subsidies theft?" Cecilia asked.

"Not that letter," he said waspishly. "It was the other letter. The one he left for Lady Aldrich."

"What other letter?"

"Mr. Miller and Mr. Oak," James suggested. "A letter hidden in a tree out past the old mill."

Cecilia's eyes widened in understanding. "When you comprehended the message about the oak tree, you went to retrieve the letter?"

"That I did, the afternoon after you all left for London."

"When you retrieved the letter, how was the letter addressed?" James asked.

"It was addressed to Lady Aldrich."

"But you opened it and read it."

The man looked away, his lips in a tight line.

"Mr. Cavanaugh?" said James.

He looked back at Sir James. "Yes, I opened the damned letter and read it," he said defiantly. "I thought it might have information I should send on to Lady Aldrich in London."

"By your failure to do that, I deduce it did not.

What did the letter say that had you convinced Lord Aldrich was party to the theft?"

"He told Lady Aldrich Lord Wheaten planned to steal government money that was for foreign countries and give it to the veterans who were more needful than foreigners. He was going to make sure the money went to the right place."

"And you assumed some of it went into his own pockets?" James suggested.

"He was always bleating about money. Gave up that cozy arrangement he had with that Sinclair woman and married trade. Theft ain't much lower than that on the scale."

"I thought you liked Lady Aldrich," Cecilia said.

Cavanaugh shrugged his shoulders slightly. "She's nice enough, but I got my reputation to look to as well."

"Your reputation?" Cecilia asked.

"My reputation as a gentleman's gentleman."

Cecilia looked confused.

"Cecilia, he means his association with trade would tarnish him for future employment opportunities."

Cecilia stared at Cavanaugh. "You can't be serious."

"And worse, he deems it appropriate to go off without me to see to him! What true gentleman does that? Hasn't the great Beau Brummell taught gentlemen better than that?"

"You are puffed up in your conceits. Beau Brummell lost his position as an arbiter of taste two years ago when he insulted Prinny," James observed drily. "Tell us the contents of the letter. What has made Lady Aldrich go tearing off in the night? I doubt she is an accomplished horsewoman to be riding in the dark. Thankfully it was near to a full moon and the sky was clear."

"He asked her to meet him at the St. Phineas the Protector church ruins on the road to Folkestone. That's what the eight days meant. Last night was the eighth night since the letter's date."

"So, was the original letter meant for Elinor or Lord Candelstone?" Cecilia asked.

"We could ask the same question of the second letter. I wonder if Aldrich expected Elinor to decipher his message, or if it weren't for Candelstone?" James said.

Cavanaugh looked from one to the other. "Who's this Lord Candelstone?"

"Lord Aldrich's employer."

"Employer? Lord Aldrich's not worked a day in his life, too indulgent for work. That one wouldn't soil his hands," he said disgustedly.

James laughed harshly. "With your attitude toward his lordship, you might wish to advertise yourself for new employment. Lord Aldrich is for King and Country—as you observed before. And I have every reason to believe he is a spy for England."

13

The Branstokes arrived at the church ruins by midafternoon. The sky was a brilliant blue with scudding white clouds, but in the distance, it looked like clouds were building, foretelling rain later in the day.

Getting down from the carriage, Cecilia turned her face up to the sun for a moment, enjoying the warmth, then turned to look at the ruin. In the clear afternoon sunlight, the ruin stood as a beautiful amalgam of gray stone, green trees, and dark shadows thrown in patterns across the soaring stone edifice. It would make for a beautiful picnic site, she thought. She remembered Elinor talking about the ruin as they drove to the cliffs, and how she and Lord Aldrich admired the area, and she wondered.

"James," she said, staring up at the vacant gothic windows. "Didn't Candelstone say something about Penwick Park being known for its folly?"

"Yes. The Penwick Park folly is on a hill and has a telescope installed. It is said that from there, with the telescope, one can see for miles around. I believe they did the sketches for one of the London Panorama exhibits from that location. Why do you ask?" he said.

"When we traveled down here before, Elinor mentioned the ruins to me. She said if she and Lord Aldrich were ever to build a folly on their property, they would both prefer a replica of an old ruin castle or church to a Greek or Roman styled folly. More romantic, they decided."

"Do you think his reference to Penwick Park could have pointed to this site?"

"I believe so. Not only did they think something like this would make a good architectural feature, this has alliteration in the naming with Penwick Park and Phineas the Protector. I think we should investigate the area," she said as she looked about.

"The ground is uneven here. It might be best if you stayed here while I search the area," James suggested.

"No, I will accompany you. Two pairs of eyes. I shall be steady enough. If not, I shall just grab tightly on to you," she said.

"And I should enjoy that," her husband teased. "But be careful. There are fallen stones lying at odd angles that you could sprain an ankle on if you were to step oddly."

"Yes, I can see that."

They picked their way through the path of fallen stones toward the nave, wide open to the sky above with patches of blue and lavender and yellow wildflowers growing among the tall grasses shadowing the rocks.

"It is so beautiful and peaceful here," Cecilia murmured. "Spiritual, though the church is long gone."

"But not so spiritual that evil stays away," James said grimly. He left Cecilia's side to walk to a pile of stones beside a half-standing wall. He bent down to pick something up, then pushed the grass away from the rocks.

"What is it, James?" Cecilia asked as she hurried toward him.

He held out a lady's glove.

"That's Elinor's!" Cecilia said.

He gestured back to the rocks. "There is evidence of blood on the rocks here. Not a lot, but it doesn't show evidence of rain or time dilution, either. It is recent."

Cecilia examined the rocks with their blood spatters. Then she looked around at the grass in the surrounding area. She found a few white threads as might come from ripped fabric. She pointed these out to James.

James looked beyond the rocks. "There is a trail," he said, pointing to the trampled grasses leading to the back of the nave.

"It looks like whoever someone injured leaned against the wall here. There is a large smear of blood. By the location of the blood, I would guess it is from an arm or shoulder wound," James said.

"Look, there is a bloody handprint." Cecilia pointed to a partial handprint.

"A man's hand."

"Yes," she agreed. "It appears Elinor bandaged whoever was injured, and then they left. I wonder if we can find traces of the direction they took?"

James glanced at the sky. "The clouds are building. We must hurry if we are to discover any signs of their direction before the weather changes and rain wipes all traces away."

"I'll own I did not pay attention to the grass as we approached."

"We will follow our trampled path out and see if we can see any other signs."

Once they left the open shell of the church and stood before it, James hailed John Coachman.

"Look about for any signs of traffic in the area. Horse or human," he called out.

His man nodded his understanding and began circling their carriage. Cecilia pointed to a small tree. "I think a horse might have been tied up over there."

"Yes, and the horse grazed here, but not for long. The grass area pulled up or eaten is not large," James observed.

"Sir James," John Coachman called out, "there're some tracks coming from the back of the church. Hard to see for the rocks."

James scanned the area again. The wind was picking up before the oncoming storm. "I think the horses went west, across the downs."

"Aye, sir, that's what I'm thinking, too," said John Coachman.

"We can't take the carriage across the downs, and a storm is coming. Let's see if we can reach The Seagull before it hits." James took Cecilia's arm and led her back to the carriage.

"What do you think, James?" Cecilia asked as John Coachman had the horses moving.

"Most likely, the same as you. Elinor found Lord Aldrich, injured, bandaged him up, and together they left the area. Where they might have gone is a mystery. I need to see a map of the area to see what is in the direction they took."

"Do you think Mr. Tinsley might have one?"

"Possibly, but maps are dear, so I hold little hope. The magistrate is the more likely owner of local maps."

"You are not thinking of riding back to Folkestone today, are you?" Cecilia asked, alarmed.

"No, and if I go see the magistrate, you will come with me. I won't leave you alone anywhere."

The fierceness in his voice drew a smile from Cecilia. She slid closer to him. He slid his arm around her. And so they stayed as the coach traveled on.

THE WIND SPIT out a warning of the advancing rainstorm as the carriage drew up before The Seagull. An ostler ran up to open the carriage door while another ran to the horses' heads. The Branstokes and John Coachman entered the inn just as the rain poured.

"Well done, John Coachman, well done," James told his old trooper. He knew his man suffered some effects from the memories of battles in Spain but had improved since he became their coachman and assumed the sobriquet *John Coachman* as his name.

"It were worrisome at times," the man admitted. "And the horses were nervous with the blowin' wind. Since there weren't no trees about, there weren't leaves nor branches blowin'. That helped."

"Get yourself a mug of ale and make sure they put it on my tab."

"Yes, sir. Thankee, sir," John Coachman said, striding toward the pub room.

"Sir James!" called out Mr. Tinsley heartily as he hurried toward them from the back of the inn. "Welcome, welcome! I have the same rooms for you as well as the private parlor. But where is the other lady? I understood from your note that she would return with you."

"We traveled separately. I had hoped she would be here before us," James said smoothly.

A strange expression traveled across the innkeeper's face. Cecilia wondered what was on his mind. She leaned against James.

"Might we go to our room now, James, you know how carriage rides so stress me, and if we are to go to Folkestone tomorrow—" she said faintly.

"Of course, dearest," her husband said, patting her arm soothingly.

"Oh, you have business in Folkestone, then?" Mr. Tinsley asked.

"I'd like to speak to Mr. Pollock more about the smugglers he mentioned."

Cecilia delicately shuddered, resuming her feigned fragility for Mr. Tinsley's benefit. "Death, and theft, and smugglers, it is not to be borne! And that monster loose in France again. It is all so distressing."

"Theft?" queried Mr. Tinsley. "Have you had a theft?"

Cecilia looked up at James. "Should I not have mentioned it? I am sorry," she asked faintly.

"It will be common knowledge soon. Do not worry yourself," James said to her. He looked at Mr. Tinsley. "The payment from the foreign office to our allies for support for their war efforts against Napoleon was stolen in route to Dover. That is why we're going to visit Mr. Pollock and enlist the services of his associates."

The color drained from Mr. Tinsley's face.

"Is something the matter, Mr. Tinsley?" James asked.

"What? No, no. It is just shocking news. But what is Mr. Pollock's involvement?"

James laughed. "The foreign office is aware of Mr. Pollock's other activities," he said drily.

"Oh." He rested a hand on the back of the chair as he took out a kerchief to wipe his brow.

"Do not worry for Mr. Pollock! The foreign office does not think there is smuggler involvement in the subsidies' theft. Rather, they would like to enlist the smugglers to find the thieves. They will offer a reward for their *anonymous* services."

"A reward, you say?" Mr. Tinsley asked.

"Yes. I am not privy to the final agreed-upon amount; however, I believe it could be upwards of ten thousand pounds," James told him.

Cecilia and James watched the play of emotions crossing Mr. Tinsley's face.

"Is something the matter, Mr. Tinsley? Do you know something?"

"Me!" squeaked the innkeeper. "No, no. Nothing, save there be smuggling. I'll own I've had a bottle or two of brandy here for the gents that hasn't come by regular commerce. Couldn't get any legally when Boney was running around, fighting everyone. But I don't ask questions, just grateful I can get some, if you know what I mean." He backed away from them as he talked, his voice harried. "Excuse me, have to check on the kitchen," he said, then turned to hurry away.

"Well, that was interesting," murmured Cecilia.

"Indeed. Come, let's get you upstairs so you can fulfill your role as sickly spouse."

Cecilia made a face. "I am regretting I ever adopted that character, no matter how useful it has been."

James laughed, but turned to lead her up the stairs. "I, however, am enjoying my role of solicitous husband. Especially when I carry you upstairs like this!" James said as he swooped her up in his arms.

"James!" Cecilia protested.

He looked down at her. "Are you really complaining?"

She lowered her lashes as she smiled. "Well, no."

"I thought not," he said as he mounted the stairs.

14

While Cecilia reluctantly rested, and since the rain had stopped and the sun had returned, James walked through the village to stretch his legs after the carriage journey. He'd walked in one direction as far as the village church when he saw John Coachman coming down the lane pushing a rickety two-wheeled cart. The cart's owner appeared to be an old woman wearing a cut-down regimental jacket. He looked to be animatedly talking to the woman, which surprised James as his man had become a taciturn fellow since a war injury caused him to walk away from battlefields and come to work for him.

"Sir James!" his coachman hailed him. "Sir James!" He started to push the cart faster to reach James; however, the woman forestalled him by the simple expedient of tugging at one fold of his voluminous driving coat.

"Easy, laddie!" James heard her crackling voice say, and immediately John Coachman stopped. He set the cart down, almost bending double over the tiny, bent woman.

John Coachman's solicitous manner toward the woman fascinated James, for it appeared so out of character for his man. He walked toward the odd couple.

"Sir James!" John Coachman said. "'Tis Mrs. Yates!"

"Git on with ye, Reuben," the woman said, calling John Coachman by his birth name. "No call for Captain Branstoke to remember nor want to!"

But James did remember her, the fierce Irish woman who stitched up and nursed many a soldier, and the woman who took up the infants of two women who died on that disastrous winter retreat over the mountains to Corunna, tying them to her back as she trudged through the snow.

"You do yourself a disservice, my dear lady," James said as he strode forward and took one of her small hands in his. "Even General Moore called you a value to the army."

She waved his compliment aside. "We did the needful," she said, blushing slightly.

"And what of Private Yates?" James asked.

"Ah, my poor Eddie, he passed on the ship within sight of England. 'Twas buried at sea."

"I am sorry to hear that. I'm surprised you didn't return to Ireland."

"I thought on that, but I've made myself useful and get by." She lifted the canvas covering her cart and picked up a doll dressed in regiment clothes. "I makes these dolls and sells them as remembrances."

He took the doll from her and turned it over in his hands. The stitching was fine and neat. "You do good work, Mrs. Yates. May I buy this from you?" He pulled his purse from his pocket. "I should like to give this to my wife." He extracted a guinea from his pocket and pressed it into her hand. Her eyes widened, but the coin quickly disappeared into the voluminous jacket she wore.

"I heard ye was married," she said. "And I was sent to find ye. I wor' scratchin' me head figuring on how to meet ye as that Mr. Tinsley don't like me coming around The Seagull, when I met Reuben here."

"Who sent you?" James asked.

"A man as took a shiv to his side, and his wife. One a my boys found them and brought them to me. He were in a bad way but I stitched him up and he's doing much better, but in no condition to go searching for ye. Lost a mite of blood."

"Lord and Lady Aldrich?" James guessed.

"Aye, that be their names," she said eagerly.

"I'd like to see them."

The woman shook her head. "I don't knows as that's be good strategy, Captain. Bad enough I seen with Reuben here, but as we know'd each other from afore, I think we get by."

"Why is that?"

"There be a pup nosin' about Dover askin' after them."

"Would that be a tall, blond gentleman, mid to late twenties, dressed plain but expensive?"

"Aye!"

"Captain Melville," James said.

"Captain, ye say? Wah!" She turned her head and spit on the ground.

James laughed.

"You won't be laughin' when I tell ye he got a fellow followin' him!"

James frowned. "No, that does create complications. I need to speak to Aldrich. It is believed he has information important to the home office."

"Important to gettin' Boney put back where he belongs?"

"Quite possibly."

She nodded. "I'll get my boys to make sure they don't come near my cottage. If ye can come at just dark, we'll squeak by."

"I didn't realize you had sons, Mrs. Yates."

She grinned. "I call the local regiment my boys. Every man jack one of 'em."

James laughed, then he spoke to John Coachman. "Get Mrs. Yates' direction, then come back to The Seagull."

"Yes, sar."

He turned again to Mrs. Yates and took one of her hands in his. "You are a treasure to the military. Until later, madam."

"MR. TINSLEY," James said as he and Cecilia descended the stairway from their room to the ground floor of The Seagull some three hours later. "I discovered earlier today a friend from my peninsular days is in the area. John Coachman brought me a message that we should visit this evening. We will not be staying for dinner, so can we have dinner here at nine?" he asked as he drew on his gloves.

"Are you still thinking to travel to Folkestone in the morning?"

"Yes, I am eager to speak with Mr. Pollock. If it weren't for the threat of smugglers that you and Pollock warn me about, we should have gone this day. I'm glad we didn't, else I would not have known about my old friend in the area."

"Who—" Mr. Tinsley began to ask.

James tucked Cecilia's arm in his. "Come, my dear," he said before Tinsley could finish his question. He knew Tinsley thought to ask the name of his friend. James saw no reason to tell him, and every reason not to. Where did Tinsley stand in this mess? He led Cecilia out of the inn.

James led Cecilia to their carriage where John Coachman waited. He helped her in, then jumped in after her. John Coachman paused at the door before closing it.

"Mrs. Yates suggested I drive a bit before taking you near her house. I won't drive the coach right to her cottage, she says as how that would cause talk."

"I've warned my wife," James said.

"Yes, and I understand," Cecilia said, leaning past James to see John Coachman. "I've on my sturdy kid half-boots," she said, kicking at her dark skirts, "so I don't mind a bit of a walk. I've been too much of a lady of leisure as it is today! And I will pull my cloak tight about me with the hood over my head so I don't stand out."

John Coachman nodded and closed the coach door. The next moment they were driving at a sedate pace out of the village and up the road toward Dover.

Mrs. Yates' cottage was not directly in Dover, but on the south-western outskirts. It was a thatched-roof cottage with a tidy garden about it. Made of loosely mortared stacked stone, it looked like a strong storm wind would blow it down. When Mrs. Yates opened the door to James' knock, Cecilia could see that the cottage was actually smaller inside than outside, for the walls were two feet thick. Dried herbs and Mrs. Yates' handmade dolls hung from the roughly hewn rafters. A fire burned greedily in the fireplace, which took up nearly one wall of the tiny cottage. A large pot hung from a hook over the fire, redolent of soup.

The cottage was square, save for the tiny, shadowed, sleeping alcove that jutted four feet out from the back of the building. In the shadows, Cecilia just made out Elinor sitting on the edge of the rope bed. She rose and walked into the light, her hands outstretched to catch Cecilia's.

"Can you ever forgive me, my dear friend, for giving your man such a turn and riding off? But if I hadn't, I don't know what would have become of Simon!" she said, looking over her shoulder at where her husband lay on the bed.

"That is something I would have done," Cecilia admitted, squeezing her friend's hands. She looked over her shoulder at her husband. "Isn't that right, James?"

James nodded, a crooked, wry smile on his lips. "Unfortunately, yes, and Cecilia warned me the day we received the letters from Pollock that you were much alike. Your loyalty is from your heart, not convention."

Behind them, they heard Lord Aldrich stirring in his bed. "Ellie!" they heard him call out. "Is someone here?"

Elinor hurried back to his bedside. "Yes, Simon, Sir James and Lady Branstoke are here. They've come to help."

Aldrich struggled to sit up.

"Don't go sittin' up!" Mrs. Yates abjured him. She hurried to reposition Elinor's rolled-up cloak behind his head as a pillow so he could at least see the Branstokes. "I've water heatin' for a tisane to get ye feelin' more the thing. Don't fratch yourself."

She raised her hand to touch his brow. He turned his head away.

Mrs. Yates clucked. "Men be all the same when they're hurtin'. Little boys!" she declared, going back to her chair by the fire.

"Oh, Simon," said Elinor, sitting down on the edge of the bed again. She laid her hand on his head. "He is much cooler now, Mrs. Yates."

Aldrich looked over at the Branstokes. "Best that you stand aside," he said, "for there was never more of a coil. Brigand against brigand against brigand."

"We know something of it through Candelstone, as I'm sure Elinor has told you. But I should like to hear from you what is going on and how you ended up stabbed," James said.

"Candelstone plays too close to fire and would have us all do so," Aldrich said harshly.

"I am all too familiar with his methods. He is a fanatic of the worst order," James said agreeably. He took Cecilia's cloak from about her shoulders and draped it on the rough-hewn oak table. Then he removed his hat and multi-caped greatcoat and laid them with her cloak. There was but one other chair in the small cottage besides the one Mrs. Yates sat in, and he pulled it forward for Cecilia. Then he stood beside her, his arms crossed over his chest.

"When Napoleon escaped from Elba," Aldrich began slowly, "our continental allies rallied to defeat him. But the foreign office knew that what they said they would do and what they would actually do could differ wildly. Our allies have felt the effects of war with Napoleon far more than we have. They are tired and disillusioned, for Napoleon's capture did not bring immediate relief to the deprivations they have experienced. Some people in Europe agitate for treaties with Bonaparte, even if there is a cost. Our government believes the cost of any treaty with Napoleon is too high.

So, to spur our allies on, Whitehall has pledged millions in foreign subsidies to bolster their convictions."

"That is essentially what Candelstone told us," James said.

"What he probably didn't tell you is the amount," Aldrich wryly said.

"He said something like one million."

Simon snorted. "At Whitehall, they've said the total for this year could come to nearly twenty million pounds!"

Cecilia and James exchanged glances. "I said before I couldn't conceive of one million pounds; I *know* I can't conceive of that much money," Cecilia said.

"While we have known for some time the various plots to steal the subsidies, most plots never make it past pints of ale discussions. Others were active. The foreign office has stopped two different groups who were well organized and past the planning stages. One of those did manage to steal some of the subsidies; however, their success was short-lived as a rival group subsequently stole the subsidies from them! The principals of both those groups have been captured," Aldrich said.

"Lord Jasper Wheaten has always objected to the vast sums meant for our allies," he continued after he took a sip of water from the cup Elinor held. "He believes these sums better spent on British subjects—particularly on the veterans disabled in wars and on the families of those soldiers killed in the wars. Righteously, he devised a plan to steal a subsidy shipment meant for Britain's allies and—Robin Hood fashion—distribute it among those in need. His plan was simple and naïve and, in its naivety, lay its success."

"He didn't see the need to steal all the funds at the same time from where they were gathered by

Rothschild. Like you, Lady Branstoke, I don't believe he could appreciate that much money. He decided one million pounds, or thereabouts, would be sufficient."

"However, Lord Wheaten is not a good judge of character. The men he approached to join him—principally Yarnell and Dunnett—did not share his world view. These men have plans of their own for the money."

"This is all in line with what Candelstone told us," James told him. "What was your role in this subsidy-stealing farce? Candelstone told us you were an innocent party who brought him news of the proposed thefts and you volunteered to spy on the group. He intimated you were a novice."

Aldrich laughed, then grimaced as laughing pulled on his side. "Hardly. I have been working for the foreign office since I came down from Oxford. I was young and idealistic and thought it all great fun to act in the role assigned to me of impecunious gentleman."

"That actually seems to be a role they like to confer," James said drily. "I know Lord Havelock had the same instruction."

"Yes, and it was a dashed nuisance. A wealthy man can act as a carefree muttonhead as well as a poor man," Aldrich grouched.

"I had my suspicions," James said. "I noted a few vacant spots on the walls at Bartlett Hall but otherwise the estate looked in good condition, not like the neglect at our Summerworth Park estate."

Aldrich grinned. "I only removed items I particularly disliked and told everyone I sold them."

"But you didn't sell them."

"No. Over his protests, I made Candelstone take

charge of them. They are wrapped in oil cloth and stored in his Dorset country house attic.".

"But what of your fortune?" Cecilia asked.

Aldrich smiled. "Safe and growing," he said.

"You did not need to marry me?" Elinor asked, her face a study of conflicting emotions.

Aldrich turned his head to her, and his smile broadened. "No, I didn't need to, but I wanted to. Remember when we met again in the fall and I said I had been thinking of you all summer?"

"Yes," she breathed.

"That was true." He pulled her hand up to his lips to kiss her palm.

James laid a hand on his wife's shoulder and squeezed gently. She looked up at him, her eyes glistening.

"Aldrich," James said, recalling him back to the matter at hand. "Why the faked carriage accident?"

The man shook his head slightly. "That was ever a farce in all ways. Yarnell was making noises to Wheaten that I was not a loyal follower of their affirmed intentions. Yarnell has always disliked me, though I don't know why, and has been suspicious," he said grimly. "Wheaten came up with the plan to stage the carriage accident. Yarnell laughed and thought that a great joke. I protested; how could I then return from the dead, and what of my new wife? Since they saw our marriage as a marriage of convenience, they did not see that as an obstacle. I couldn't persuade them away from this plan. I asked if I could write a note to my wife and leave it in the portmanteau to certify my identity and to communicate to Elinor again. They agreed, so I wrote the letter, Yarnell breathing over my shoulder as I wrote. It wasn't a particularly clever letter, but I hoped someone could sort out some of the meaning to get word to Candelstone."

"So you meant to have the letter go to Candelstone?"

"Yes."

James laughed harshly. "I'm afraid we thwarted you on that. Candelstone sent Captain Melville to follow up on any communications you might have with Elinor. He was such a ham-handed idiot that he drove Cecilia to dislike and mistrust him, therefore we were not inclined to give him anything."

Aldrich smirked. "He tries too hard. He desperately wants to be as legendary with the home office as his late brother-in-law, Lord Blessingame."

"I agree," James said. "But back to the carriage. The accident, as staged, was not believable. No blood and no bodies. The horses, still in harness, were found grazing nearby, the shaft obviously sawed."

Aldrich nodded. "Yes. Yarnell was angry as to how it was done; luckily, I had nothing to do with that, and have not seen what they did. Lord Wheaten arranged it all."

"Lord Wheaten!" Elinor exclaimed. "But he was so nice to me when he visited. How could he do that to me?"

Her husband patted her hand. "He is a fanatic, my dear. The ends justify the means." He looked up at James. "And the irony is he hired smugglers to do it!" he explained.

James shook his head in disgust. "And since the smugglers report to Pollock..."

"Ah, so you know that," Aldrich interjected.

"I've inferred that," he said. "I've been to Pollock's house. The art objects alone tell a different story than him being a simple country gentleman and magistrate. Then there are his staff members. His butler is a bruiser. If I wasn't certain after that visit, some things Candelstone said confirmed my suspicions."

"Pollock walks a fine line," Aldrich said.

"So, he does. Now we come to your injury."

Aldrich frowned. "That was my stupidity and reaffirms why Candelstone does not like married or otherwise attached agents. To be blunt, I wanted to see Elinor," he said, taking her hand in his. "I was hoping Mrs. Wembly would tell her about the old message tree."

"Unfortunately, she didn't," Elinor said sadly.

"However, she told Mr. Cavanaugh," said Cecilia.

"And Cavanaugh has now decided he wants a piece of the action. He's quite put out with you," James added.

"So Elinor has told me," Aldrich said darkly.

"Did you know he feels working for you, now that you have married Elinor, is likely to devalue him as an employee to others?" Cecilia asked.

"What nonsense is that?"

"As her father is in trade, he thinks that hurts his reputation as a gentleman's gentleman," Cecilia said.

"I hope you will forgive me; however, I suggested to the man that he should find alternate employment," James said carefully.

Aldrich gave a short laugh. "Thank you! Hopefully he will take your suggestion, saving me from firing him. But enough about Cavanaugh. You want to know about the knife in my side."

Cecilia and James nodded.

"Since I didn't know when Elinor would get the message, every night that I could, I went out to the church ruins. Yarnell followed me that last night. He caught me by surprise. I had just realized Elinor had come, so my attention was on her and not on my surroundings, as they should have been. Yarnell snuck up on me, intending to stab me in the back. At the last moment, I sensed his presence and turned so his knife only caught my side. The noise of our scuffle caught Elinor's attention. She came running up and Yarnell took off. Elinor bandaged me up as best she could, and we made our way toward Dover, going across the downs. I warned her I was near to passing out. Would you believe this wonderful wife of mine hitched up her skirts and climbed up behind me on my horse, holding me in place until we came to a small farm?"

"Yes, I would," declared Cecilia, smiling at her friend.

Elinor looked down, her cheeks blushing.

"The tenants brought me in a wagon to Mrs. Yates, who they said was the best surgeon for injuries because of her experience in the wars."

"That was lucky for us," said Cecilia.

"But now what?" James asked. "Do you know where the subsidies are hidden?"

"I know where they were; they were in the Woodhaven Manor stables."

"Woodhaven Manor?" James asked.

"That is the home of Lord Wheaten's sister. She suffers from dementia and he had her placed in an asylum last February. He has been working with her lawyers to see what to do about the estate, but in the meantime, he deemed it a perfect location for the subsidies. But the guns and gold may not still be there. Yarnell and Dunnett don't like that location. It is too far from the water. They want everything moved to the Western Heights," Aldrich explained.

"The Western Heights? But isn't that an army barracks?" James asked.

Aldrich grimaced and shifted a bit in the bed, to get more comfortable. "Partly," he said. "But it is huge, a rabbit-warren of tunnels and rooms for storing munitions, not all interconnected. Dunnett knows of an area that has been dug but has not yet had the revetment completed. Evidently, they abandoned work on it several years ago for work on the North Center Bastion instead."

"What is a revetment?" Elinor asked.

"A brick lining for the tunnel," her husband explained, then he continued. "It horrified Wheaten to learn some of the subsidies are in weapons. Got quite shrill and frightened. My guess is Dunnett and Yarnell are thinking to the sell the weapons to the French."

"Interesting. But what about the partnership they have with each other?"

Aldrich shrugged slightly.

Mrs. Yates got up from her chair where she had been listening to Lord Aldrich's story. "Is that Dunnett Captain Dunnett?" she asked.

"Yes, madam," James said.

She shook her head. "Now there's a piece of filth that could have been left on the battlefield," she grumbled. "But if he knows where these tunnels are that you say they will hide their loot in, then no doubt some of my boys knows 'em, too."

"That is likely true," Aldrich said consideringly. "I doubt Dunnett has ever gone exploring himself; that would get his boots and jacket dirty."

Mrs. Yates gave a cackle of laughter.

"Can you ask around of your boys, Mrs. Yates?"

"Aye, that I can. I see Sergeant Major Kendall first thing tomorrow. He'll know or know who does."

"Excellent. If he does, can you ask him to meet me here tomorrow evening?" James asked.

"Meet *us* here," Cecilia corrected.

James looked down at her. "No, Cecilia," he said, his expression implacable.

She merely raised an eyebrow in return.

"We should go now. If you need to reach us, please do so through John Coachman," James said.

"Who?" Mrs. Yates said.

James smiled. "Reuben," he corrected.

"Oh, aye, that I will indeed."

"Aldrich," James said. "I'll see you tomorrow."

15

"Mr. Tinsley may ask questions on our return, all in a friendly, talkative manner," James said to Cecilia as John Coachman drove them back to The Seagull. "I haven't figured out if he is involved with Lord Wheaten, the smugglers, or perhaps both."

Cecilia nodded from where she sat in the circle of his arm. "I know. I have wondered the same. And when I think of what happened the night you were in Folkestone, I wonder if his allegiance could be to whoever pays him the most!"

"You think Melville paid him to allow that break-in to your room?" James asked. He felt her nod again against his shoulder. "I hadn't previously considered that as a possibility. It is worth bearing in mind." He pulled her closer to his side. "A man whose loyalty is to whoever last crossed his palm with silver is a dangerous man. There is no predicting how he might act. I'd rather encounter a villain who I knew was out to steal my purse than to be around someone who I couldn't tell if he were friend or foe."

"Yes," Cecilia agreed, "so we should agree on our evening's activities."

She felt more than heard his soft chuckle.

"I think we can honestly say we have been to visit Mrs. Yates," he said. "She is well known in the area, and I knew her in Spain. We can say John Coachman discovered her while walking about, which is true. We do not need to provide any other information beyond memories of people and events from our time in the same regiment."

"Simple is better."

James nodded. "If the weather holds up, I'm going to see if Mr. Tinsley has a tilbury we might rent for the trip to Folkestone. I'd rather leave our traveling carriage and John Coachman here in case Mrs. Yates needs to communicate with us."

"I should like a drive in a carriage from where I can see the area better. And we can bring our umbrellas and cloaks should the weather turn," Cecilia said.

Just then, John Coachman drove the carriage under the arch before The Seagull, into the courtyard with its blaze of lights.

"That was a much faster trip back than when we left!" observed Cecilia.

James nodded. "Remember, he drove a circuitous route to get us to Mrs. Yates' cottage. I did not think we needed to do that returning to The Seagull," James told her.

As before, the door to the carriage flew open the instant the carriage stopped, and an ostler was setting the steps. James descended first, then turned to help Cecilia.

Inside the inn tavern, a crowd of young gentlemen were drinking and singing bawdy songs.

"James," Cecilia said softly, "I'm going to go on up to the small parlor. Can you request Mr. Tinsley to have a light supper served there?"

"Yes, my dear."

He watched her make her way up the stairs, then turned to look for Mr. Tinsley.

He walked toward the blowsy middle-aged barmaid distributing beer to the frolicking gentlemen. He was almost at her side when he recognized one reveler as Bishop Yarnell.

"Excuse me, miss," he said, his eyes gliding over Yarnell as if he didn't know him. "Where might I find Mr. Tinsley?" he asked, his focus on her.

"He be in his office, sar, tucked back unner the stairs there," she said, pointing to a dark hall that ran next to the stairs.

"Thank you," he said.

"Excuse me, sar," she said as he would turn toward the office. "You be the gent wif the misses as wants a late supper in the upstairs parlor?" she asked.

"Yes."

She nodded. "I was to tell ya if I seen ya that it will be sent up directly like."

"Excellent. My wife is quite hungry and will be grateful for the meal," James told her, pleased Tinsley remembered his request for a later dinner.

He walked down the hallway next to the stairs, not looking back at Yarnell or any of the other men in his company. He knocked on the door he found tucked in the back corner.

"Come in!" he heard through the door.

James opened the door to find Mr. Tinsley with an accounting ledger opened before him. He closed it when he saw James.

"I told Ruby, the barmaid, to be on the lookout for you. She's having your supper sent up to you."

"Yes, I have spoken with her. I have another mission in speaking to you."

"Yes," Mr. Tinsley said, suspicion narrowing his eyes.

James laughed at his expression. "A money-making mission for you," he said.

Tinsley relaxed back in his chair. "Sorry, sure. How can I help you?" He indicated with a wave of his hand an invitation to sit down.

James took the seat in front of the large oak desk. "Where can I rent a tilbury or other small carriage for early tomorrow morning?" he asked. He crossed one booted foot over his other knee.

"You're thinking to drive to Folkestone?" Tinsley asked.

"Yes. My wife is tired of riding in closed carriages. I told her if the weather held, we can drive to Folkestone in an open carriage."

"We have both a curricle and a tilbury," Tinsley said, relaxing back in his chair.

"Do they both have bonnets?" James asked.

"No, only the tilbury has."

James nodded. "Then that is the one I should hire in case the weather does kick up a rainstorm."

"Excellent, sir. At what time would you like to have it ready?" the innkeeper asked.

Frowning, James considered for a moment. "I should say nine in the morning."

"So you will want breakfast at eight?" Tinsley dipped his quill in the inkwell and jotted down some notes.

"Yes. I'm giving my John Coachman the day off, but please see anything he needs here is put on my tab."

Tinsley nodded. "I should be delighted, sir."

James laughed then. He straightened in his chair.

"Though I doubt you will see much of him. He has discovered an old friend in Dover."

"As did you!" Mr. Tinsley observed. He replaced the quill in the inkwell.

"Yes, someone from our old regiment," James said, smiling.

"I know many of the older campaigners. Who might that be, if I might ask?" he said, leaning forward to rest his elbows on the desk.

"Mrs. Yates."

"The doll-maker?" Tinsley frowned. "She is a mite tetched now, you know."

James frowned. "No, I didn't know. We visited her this evening and did not find any fault in her. My wife was quite entranced with her stories."

"To be sure, to be sure," Mr. Tinsley hastily said. "However, the woman is known for her confabulations. I would listen to what she says with half an ear," he said with a forced laugh.

"I'm sorry to hear that. I'll let John Coachman know." James stood up.

"Yes, sir. And we will have the carriage ready for you promptly at nine," Tinsley said, rising as well.

"Thank you," James said as he turned to leave. At the door, he stopped and turned back to Mr. Tinsley. "Please don't be offended if you see John Coachman inspecting the tilbury and the horse carefully before we depart. It is just his way," he said.

※

"WHAT TOOK YOU SO LONG?" Cecilia asked when he finally joined her in the private parlor.

"I was speaking with Tinsley to order a carriage for us in the morning. He says he has a tilbury available."

"Excellent!"

"And I will have John Coachman examine it in the morning before we leave," James added.

Cecilia's eyes widened. "You think someone would try to sabotage our carriage?"

"No; however, before I left Tinsley, I told him not to be surprised if John Coachman inspected the carriage and horse. I don't know why I felt the need to say that, but when I threw that out, his expression gave me pause. Maybe I said it because I saw Bishop Yarnell in that group of men in the tavern."

"Mr. Yarnell is here? Is he staying here?"

"He is here with the loud crowd below; however, whether he is staying here, I cannot say."

"Most interesting," she said. "But come and eat and I shall tell you of my conversation with Daphne Tinsley as it was she who brought our supper upstairs."

"Did you discuss Mrs. Yates?"

"Yes. She quite likes the woman but says her father doesn't and won't let her come around the inn," she said as she removed the covers from their food.

"Why not?" James poured ale from a pitcher into mugs for them.

"Because she is too quiet."

James looked quizzically at her. "Too quiet?"

She nodded. "He thinks she is too nosy, always watching and listening. Doesn't say much but seems to be always around. Her silence and her slight smile make him nervous."

He passed a mug to her. "That is interesting," he drawled. "I wonder what he has to hide."

"That was my thought. It also seems as perhaps we should have been questioning Mrs. Yates more. The entire time we talked to Lord Aldrich, she sat and listened," Cecilia said. She took a bite of stew.

"Do not refine too much on that," James said. "As a camp follower, she would have learned to keep quiet."

Cecilia considered that as she chewed her food. "I quite see that; however, I am also certain she knows more than she lets on. It also could be she knows more than she realizes she does. I wish we had asked her about the smugglers and their potential involvement with the subsidy's theft. She might have an interesting perception."

"I'm more inclined to believe she has a clear vision of who is honest and who is not while I struggle with nuances," James said as he buttered a slice of bread.

They ate together in companionable silence. "She sees things clearer?" Cecilia suggested. "Right or wrong? Black or white, no gray?"

"That would be my thought."

"What is gray in all of this for you?" she asked him.

"Lord Wheaten. He is a fanatic; however, his fanaticism is for those he deems less fortunate than himself. Yes, he wants to steal the subsidies and distribute them, Robin Hood fashion, across the country." He finished his bread and washed it down with ale. "The country has put a tax on practically everything to raise the funds for our military and for buying these subsidy payments. Those taxes hit everyone one, rich or poor. His approach is wrong; however, I can't help but laud him for his ideals."

Cecilia touched her napkin to her lips. "Sadly, idealists don't live in reality," she said.

He nodded. "And idealists can get people hurt," he said. He pushed his chair back from the table. "I'm for bed. It has been a long day and we will face an even longer one tomorrow." He held out his hand to her. She placed her hand in his and rose from her chair.

"Now that we have found Lord Aldrich and met with him, I hope we are nearing the end of our inquiry."

"As do I, my dear; I'd like to return to discussions of estate improvements. Far less fatiguing than this affair."

Cecilia laughed. "Oh, do not prevaricate to me! I know you are enjoying this investigation. It appeals to your inquisitive nature."

He shrugged slightly, but when he looked down at his wife, his expression reflected a rueful smile.

MUCH TO CECILIA'S DELIGHT, the weather cooperated and only a few clouds marred the beautiful blue expanse of the morning sky, and the carriage moved along at a nice pace toward Folkestone. She and James had fallen into a companionable silence.

Cecilia would have loved to turn her face up to the warmth of the sun, but how detrimental that would be to her complexion! She contented herself with looking out across the landscape. Sometimes she saw the sea to their left, other times a wide expanse of grasses with wildflowers tucked in the folds of the low chalk hills around them.

She felt the carriage slowing and turned her head to look down the road. Ahead, blocking the road, were four men on horseback, one with a rifle, the other three with pistols drawn.

"James?" she whispered.

"I don't think we are going to make Folkestone today," he said as he brought the carriage to a halt. "You have your lavender water with you?"

She turned her head to look at him as the four men rode toward them. "Yes, and *sal volatile*," she whispered, understanding that he foresaw the need for her ruse.

He nodded slightly, not taking his eyes off the men that approached them. "The one riding toward us on the right is Bishop Yarnell. Interesting, the man just after him looks like Mr. Pollock's butler, Bernard."

"Bernard Oakes?" Cecilia asked.

"At this point, I would assume so. Pollock only called him Bernard. I don't know the others."

She recognized one man as Daphne's young man, Stephen, who boarded up the window during their last stay at the inn. "The youngest works for Mr. Tinsley," she said.

"Hmm, interesting," he murmured.

"Yarnell," James called out as they drew nearer. "Is something the matter?"

"You are what is the matter," Yarnell said as he rode up next to the tilbury.

"James" Cecilia said weakly, her voice quavering. "What is going on?" She held her eyes wide open as she looked from Yarnell to the others in the group.

Yarnell bowed slightly toward her. "My lady, you are heading in the wrong direction."

"I don't understand. James!" she cried out as she turned to her husband and clung to his arm.

"Hush, my dear," James said, patting her hand. "I believe Mr. Yarnell does not want us to be visiting Mr. Pollock."

"Very good, Sir James, very good," said Yarnell. "Now, sir, you will turn your carriage around and come with us."

"Where are we going?" James asked. Beside him, Cecilia clung tighter to his arm.

"Why, to an old manor house close to here, owned by Lord Wheaten, Woodhaven Manor. I'm sure you know Wheaten," he said affably enough, though his expression did not match. "Everyone knows Wheaten, with his high ideals," Yarnell said with a laugh. "Turn the horses about," he continued, his tone harsher.

"James, I'm frightened! I think I'm going to faint!" Cecilia exclaimed.

"Not now, Cecilia," James said as he pulled the reins to turn the equipage. "I suggest you pull out your *sal volatile* if your feel unwell."

"Oh, don't be so heartless. You know how fragile my constitution is. I cannot take stress. I don't understand what is going on!" she flung at him.

Yarnell laughed while he backed his horse away so James could turn the carriage. "How did you come to be leg-shackled to this one?" he asked.

James sighed. "It seemed like a good idea at the time."

"James!" wailed Cecilia.

"Cecilia!" James said harshly.

She slumped against him, her lips pouting. She wished she could do tears on command, but she had not mastered that attribute. With her head slightly down, she studied the men who were with Yarnell.

Young Stephen looked uncomfortable and unsure of the situation, for he kept turning his head toward the other three men, but the man James didn't know appeared as hard and as confident as Yarnell. He must be Captain Dunnett.

Two miles down the road, Yarnell had James turn down a lane that edged a small chalk escarpment that looked like one side of a hill slipped down from the other. As they rounded the curve of the hill, Cecilia could see a small valley densely forested. The lane they drove down led to a red brick manor. A dog barked and ran toward the carriage. Yarnell leaned down to swat at him with his riding crop.

"Get out of here!" he commanded, the crop connecting with the dog's head. The dog yelped and dodged away.

"Stupid animal," Yarnell growled.

Yarnell directed James to drive to the stables. Inside, he ordered them out of the tilbury. Cecilia looked wide-eyed about her, clinging to James as he helped her down from the carriage.

In a corner of the large stable, near a large pile of hay, were stacks of wooden crates, the top boards pried loose on a few. Cecilia assumed those were from the subsidies. It didn't look like such a large number of crates that they could hold the value Lord Aldrich assigned to them. She let her eyes slide away from them and instead pressed her face into James' chest. With her hand wrapped around his arm, she tried to indicate the direction of the crates. He looked down at her and nodded slightly.

Yarnell pushed them toward the stable doors.

"What is the meaning of this, Yarnell? You have interrupted our journey to Folkestone, frightened my wife, and brought us to some unknown manor in the countryside. What is your purpose?" James asked, sounding irritated, not angry.

Yarnell pushed them again. Cecilia stumbled, but James caught her.

"Is that necessary?" James asked, irritation giving way to anger.

Yarnell laughed. "Have done, Sir James, you have been found out."

"What are you talking about?"

Yarnell smirked. "Candelstone was seen talking with you at White's, then he is at your home the next morning. Now what would Candelstone want with the enigmatic, bored Sir James Branstoke? Nothing! Unless, I'm thinking, said enigmatic, bored Sir James Branstoke is really an agent of the home office."

"What?" Cecilia exclaimed before she could stop herself.

Yarnell ignored her. "And I asked around about you. You are supposed to be in Scotland on your honeymoon."

"Plans change," James said evenly, "and you are shooting wide of the mark."

"I don't think so, but I'm not taking any chances. I have too much riding on this endeavor. It is too bad you thought to bring your wife with you. And such a pretty little thing she is, too. Such a shame. Move, walk toward the manor," he said, prodding James' shoulder with his pistol.

"Where are you taking us? What are you doing?" said Cecilia plaintively.

"Just putting you away where you won't be a bother to me," Yarnell said. Behind him followed Dunnett and Stephen. Bernard Oakes stayed in the stable to unhitch the tilbury and turn the horse out.

He directed them to the back servants' entrance of the manor and once inside, down a flight of stone stairs to the cellar, where the glow of a lantern beckoned.

When they entered the lantern glow, Cecilia realized they were in the servants' dining hall. A trestle table took up most of the space in the room. On one side of the table was a long bench, on the other side, and at the ends were wooden chairs. Two other people were before them down here, and they were tied to the chairs they sat in.

"Lord Wheaten!" James exclaimed.

"Shut up!" Yarnell ordered. "Stephen, you take Lady Branstoke and tie her up over here," Yarnell said, pointing to a chair away from the others along the wall. "Dunnett, search Sir James for any hidden knives or other weapons, then secure Sir James in the chair at this end of the table. Make sure the knots are tight."

Dunnett smiled. "With pleasure."

"James!" Cecilia cried out as Stephen pulled her away from her husband.

Stephen sat her in the chair and had her put her hands behind her back. "I'm right sorry," Stephen said softly as he wrapped a rope around her wrists.

"Do you think he is going to kill us?" she whispered to the young man. She saw him look in Yarnell's direction.

"I don't know," he said. "But I know I won't." He wrapped the rope around her body, but he handed her a length of rope to hold, and then he knelt down and tied her ankles together over her gown and then to the chair legs. Cecilia was aware he was not tying her knots tightly, but she whimpered as if they were cutting into her fair skin.

More than ever, she wished she could cry on demand. Maybe if she thought of something that would make her sad. She thought of Elinor and when she received the news of her husband's death. She imagined herself in Elinor's position and receiving news of James' death. A deep black hollowness grew in her chest. She felt tears trickle down her cheeks.

"Cecilia!" James said.

Mutely, she shook her head.

"Gag him," Yarnell ordered Dunnett.

"Why? No one can hear him down here," Dunnett challenged as he straightened from tying his legs.

"Because I told you to!" shouted Yarnell. "And hurry up. We have to get the rest of those crates loaded onto wagons so we can move them tonight. I don't like them this far from the coast. Harder to transport to sea. Damn Pollock and his sudden scruples. He'd transport gold anywhere for a price, but he won't transport guns. This entire plan has been one foul-up after another. First the government using some of the gold to buy guns for the allies, then that damned banker dividing the shipments up between ports. What the bloody hell was that about?"

"We will still have plenty with the gold and the weapon sales. Those Baker rifles alone will fetch more in gold than the government spent on them," Dunnett said.

Yarnell snorted. "So, you say," Yarnell growled as he turned toward the stairs. "Stephen, grab that lantern as you come."

"No!" Cecilia cried out plaintively.

Stephen looked at her, stricken. "I'm sorry, my lady. I'll come and release you when this is all over—somehow." He grabbed the lantern and turned to go.

Cecilia looked around the room as the moving lantern illuminated it. There was another lantern by the fireplace, and candles on a sideboard along with a wick trimmer and candle snuffer. She didn't see a flint, but with those items in the room, the tools to light a fire should be here as well.

16

After Stephen climbed the stairs and closed the door above, the room plunged into absolute darkness.

Cecilia tried opening her eyes wider, but the darkness didn't change. She shivered, not from coldness in the air, but the feeling of oppressive heaviness in the darkness touching her skin.

Lord Wheaten whimpered and moaned.

"I should never have trusted that Yarnell fellow. I should have listened to Lord Aldrich. I just wanted some of that money to stay in England and benefit our veterans," he whined.

"It is okay, Lord Wheaten. Do not fret over what is done. We need to think of how we can get out of here and stop Yarnell and Dunnett," Cecilia said calmly, all traces of the hysterical woman gone. "Do you know if there is flint and steel in this room?"

"No-o-o," he said, his voice shaking.

"I believe there is a brass-lined wooden box on the mantel shelf with char cloth, flint and steel, my lady," said the crisp voice of Lord Wheaten's man.

"Thank you, sir. And what is your name?" Cecilia asked the strangely disembodied voice.

"Jeffers, my lady, Lionel Jeffers."

"Thank you, Mr. Jeffers."

"But what is the use? They tied us up and they took the lantern," Wheaten whined.

James made a muffled, harsh noise behind his gag.

"Yes, James," Cecilia said, addressing her husband. "I am working on it."

"Working on what?" Mr. Jeffers asked.

"Stephen did not bind me tightly. I believe I can get loose," she said as she worked on the knots around her wrists. The loop of rope Stephen put in her hand allowed her to keep her hands more apart. Because of that extra length of rope, she could get her hands far enough apart to bend her wrists so the fingers of one hand could feel the knots and slowly work to unravel them. She closed her eyes. She didn't know how it was that it felt better to close her eyes to concentrate when it was already pitch-black in the room, but closing her eyes helped her fingers *see* better. The rough rope scraped her skin and broke her fingernails, but with patience, she felt the knots loosen.

Suddenly, the rope dropped to the floor.

"What was that?" Lord Wheaten asked, startled and fearful.

"Freedom," Cecilia said. She bent over to free her ankles. The fact that young Stephen tied them over her skirts in concession to a woman's modesty made them easy for Cecilia to push down from her calves to the floor. She stepped out of the circle of rope. She opened her eyes.

The room was still pitch-black. She felt turned around and directionless. She stood still for a moment to remember the room layout in the lantern light.

"James?" she called out into the darkness.

James thumped his chair against the stone floor.

Cecilia turned toward his thumps and slowly made her way toward him. It seemed like an eternity before her questing hands brushed his jacket. She traced his shoulders to his neck, to the gag across his mouth. She couldn't untie the knot, but she could push the gag down, away from his mouth.

"Thank you," he managed, his voice a dry croak.

She grabbed his face in the dark and kissed him, and then she felt down his arms to where his hands were tied. The knots were tight, and she felt how they were tied in the dark. "I need a knife, or a light, or both!" she said as she examined the ropes with her fingertips.

"Straight behind me should be the fireplace," James said.

"Yes, I remember." She hesitated to leave his side; the dark was so intense. But the fireplace shouldn't be more than four or five feet away. She walked forward, hoping she was moving in a straight line, but in the darkness, she couldn't gauge straight or curved.

"Ouch!" Cecilia cried out when her foot stumbled against the hearthstone before she found the mantel with her hands.

"Cecilia?" James asked.

"I'm okay," she assured him. She ran her fingertips across the fireplace and found a rectangular wood box. She opened it. Feeling inside the box, she discovered it had two compartments. She felt a piece of flint, a steel striker, and a bit of cloth. She closed the box to keep the contents safe in the dark, then searched with her hands across the mantel for the candle she had seen there earlier. With her mantel discoveries clutched close to her, she eased herself down on the floor before the hearth.

"What are you doing?" James asked.

"I'm sitting on the floor. The mantel is too high for me to work from."

"Just don't light a fire in the hearth," he warned.

"Why not?"

"If Yarnell and Dunnett have not left the area yet, they may see the smoke."

"I had not thought of that, and I *was* thinking to light a fire. All right." She carefully opened the tinderbox again. One side held the flint and the curved steel striker. The other side she felt gritty char cloth and pieces of fiber that felt like unwound rope. She placed a piece of the gritty cloth on the flint, then forcefully brought the striker down. She missed the flint. "Oh gracious," she muttered.

"You do know my anxiety for you is increasing, don't you?" James said in a conversational tone.

"You don't have anxiety," Cecilia said as she determinedly brought the striker down again. This time she struck it. There was a spark, but it winked out of existence almost immediately. Heartened, Cecilia tried again. This time the char cloth took a spark. She blew on the cloth gently as she pulled a piece of the fibrous material from the box and brought it up to the spark. She blew gently again, and smoke came off the fiber. She tried again, and the fiber whooshed into a small flame. Quickly she brought the candlewick to the flame and was gratified to see it light. She dropped the small flaming fiber on the hearthstone and it immediately extinguished.

"Well done, my lady," said Jeffers.

"Yes, my dear. Well done," said James.

"Thank you," Cecilia said as she carefully stood up with the candle in hand. She then picked up a lantern from the floor and lit the wick, bringing the lantern and the candle to the table.

"There will be knives in the sideboard," offered Mr. Jeffers.

Holding the candle, she crossed to the sideboard and found several knives in a drawer, along with a candlestick on the top of the sideboard. She jammed the candle into the holder and grabbed one of the knives. With adequate light and a proper tool, she felt excitement ripple through her. She returned to where James was tied up. She knelt on the floor and set the candlestick beside her.

"My arms and legs have gone numb," Lord Wheaten said, whining again.

"I'm not surprised," Cecilia said as she studied the multiple knots on James' bindings. "Captain Dunnett was determined you wouldn't get free," she said to her husband. "You shouldn't have tried to work your way free. Your wrists are rubbed raw."

"Can you not free me first?" whined Wheaten.

Cecilia glanced in his direction. "I could, but I won't. It was your actions that caused the mess we find ourselves in.

"But—"

"No!" she said as she sawed at the knots binding James.

"Don't use the knife like a saw. It will dull too fast. Use a smooth stroke," James instructed. "The rope will cut easier."

Cecilia changed her cutting action to smooth, one-way strokes. "Yes, this is better, but it takes so long to cut through his mess."

"Perseverance, my love, like the candle spark," he said calmly.

She nodded. "I know." She bit her lower lip as she worked on the rope. Behind her, she heard Lord Wheaten and his valet talking quietly. She didn't pay them any heed, though it seemed Wheaten had taken his complaints to his valet, which was fine with Cecilia.

"Almost through," Cecilia finally said to James.

He strained to pull his hands apart as she cut. Suddenly, the last of the rope fibers broke apart.

"Ah!" he said in relief. He massaged his wrists, one after the other. "Thank you. Were there more knives where you found this one?"

"Yes."

"Good, then give me this knife. I'll work on my ankles, and you can start on Lord Wheaten and his man."

"Must I?" she whispered in his ear.

He smiled and kissed her cheek. "I understand, but yes," he said.

Cecilia grabbed another knife from the sideboard drawer and then quickly freed first Lord Wheaten and then Mr. Jeffers.

"You should have released me first. I need to get that gold!" Lord Wheaten said.

"I beg your pardon," Cecilia said. In the dimly lit room, it was hard to see Lord Wheaten's face, but his voice reverberated with the passion.

"I need to get that gold from Yarnell and Dunnett. I don't care about the weapons, they can keep them, but I need the gold for the soldiers! We must hurry!"

"How dare you!" Cecilia said. "I should never have untied you."

"It's no use, miss," said Mr. Jeffers sadly. "This whole plan has been a disaster and hard on Lord Wheaten. He's a good man at heart, but this last year with his sister's increasing infirmities and the couple mild apoplectic fits he has suffered, the stress has damaged his common sense. And two days ago, he suffered a far stronger apoplectic fit. He ain't been right since."

"His manner reminds me of what happened with my father's old estate steward, Mr. Lincoln," James said, coming up to them. "Lord Wheaten needs a direction, actions to cling to."

He put his hand on Lord Wheaten's shoulder, drawing his attention. "Lord Wheaten, the government is offering a ten thousand pound reward for information about the subsidy theft. You could claim that reward for your soldiers."

"I could?"

"Yes, but only if you act fast. You must go to Folkestone and tell the magistrate there what is going on and get his help to capture Yarnell and Dunnett. You do that, and I'll speak to the government on your behalf."

"All right! Must go to Folkestone. Hear that, Jeffers? We must go to Folkestone and tell the magistrate. Must go." He stood up and shuffled toward the stairs, only to stop halfway there. "Jeffers! Why is it so dark?" Lord Wheaten complained.

Cecilia picked up the lantern and handed it to the valet, then took the candlestick for her and James.

"You go before us," the valet said. "It might take a while to get him upstairs," he explained sadly.

"Thank you," Cecilia said.

James laid a light hand on her back as he guided her forward. "Your man has the lantern," he told Wheaten as they passed him.

"Good, good," Wheaten wheezed. He leaned against the wall.

"I've got you, sir," they heard the valet say as Cecilia gathered up her skirts and they ran up the stairs ahead of them.

Cecilia eagerly reached to open the door latch, but James grabbed her hand and pulled her away.

"What?" she asked.

"Smoke," he said.

Then she smelled it and saw it curl out from under the door toward them.

He put the flat of his hand on the thick door. "Bloody hell! It's warm to the touch," he told her. "There is a fire on the other side; we can't get out that way."

"What are we going to do?" she asked as they started back down the steps.

"Find out what Wheaten and Jeffers know about this house, if there is another entrance, or perhaps a dug-out cold storage area where we can take refuge. The fire most likely won't burn there. The biggest problem might be a lack of air in a space like that."

"Then let's hope for another way out," Cecilia said, hurrying down the steps. The smell of smoke grew stronger, and she could hear flames crackle.

"Sir James?" asked Jeffers. He had managed to climb four steps with Lord Wheaten.

"Mr. Jeffers," James said, "we can't get out that way. You will need to take Lord Wheaten back down the stairs."

A loud bang reverberated across the ceiling. Cecilia felt her heart pound harder and faster. She remembered being in the hold of the burning ship. No, not again. She grabbed her husband's arm.

"Why can't we get out that way, is the door locked?" Jeffers asked. "I think I might have a key—"

"No, it is not locked," James said grimly. "They've set the house on fire."

"What! Bloody hell! What are we going to do?"

"What is going on?" Lord Wheaten asked.

"The house is on fire and we can't get out," Jeffers told him.

"But we have to," Lord Wheaten said. "We have to go to Folkestone. Sir James said so."

"I'm sorry, my lord," James said gently as he got on the other side of Lord Wheaten and helped Jeffers get the man back down the stairs.

"What other chambers are down here?" James asked Mr. Jeffers when they reached the bottom of the stairs. They guided Lord Wheaten to a chair.

"Besides this room, only the butler's room and the housekeeper's room, that I know of," Jeffers said. "I have spent little time here and certainly had no occasion other than meals to come down here. I didn't explore."

"What is he doing?" Cecilia asked.

"What?" James said, turning toward her.

"Lord Wheaten," she said, pointing to Lord Wheaten. He'd gotten up from the chair and was shuffling toward a low door under the stairs that they hadn't noted before.

James went to the man's side. "Lord Wheaten, what's beyond that door?"

"Coal."

"Coal?"

"She asked me for it. I thought it clever of her to think of it. Clever puss, my sister. Where is she?" He turned to look around the room.

"Lord Wheaten, what did you have put in?"

Wheaten frowned at James. "Coal bins, of course. Just like my London house."

James turned toward Cecilia and Jeffers. "We have our way out."

17

James opened the low door. He had to crouch to go through the entry. Three feet beyond the door, he could dimly make out a wall of coal.

"Jeffers, the lantern, please," James said, backing out of the small area.

Jeffers passed it to him.

"We are going to need to dig through the coal to reach the hatch door above. I couldn't see it, but I would guess it is at least ten feet beyond this door to the servants hall."

Another crash from above had them looking at the ceiling. The room was growing warm.

"We don't have time to waste," Cecilia said as she brushed past James to walk into the coal bin. She was short enough to pass under the door lintel without bending.

She started pulling coal toward her, her actions causing more coal to roll down the pile. James came up to her side.

"Let me," he said. "You hold the lantern."

"I can help!"

"I need the light, and I have longer arms and bigger hands than you," he countered as he passed her the lantern. There was already black coal dust streaking her dress. "Shine the lantern up, see if you can find the door."

She held the lantern up as high as she could and stood on tiptoes to stretch farther. "Yes! I see it," she said. She turned to where Jeffers and Wheaten stood in the doorway. "Mr. Jeffers, isn't there a coal scuttle and shovel by the fireplace? Please fetch them!"

Jeffers nodded and let go of Lord Wheaten's elbow.

When he brought the items to them, Cecilia passed the shovel to her husband.

"Please bring Lord Wheaten in here. We are going to need to move the coal behind us to get to the door. I don't want him to be on the other side." She coughed at the rising coal dust from her husband's digging and shoveling coal.

James paused in pulling down the mountain of coal ahead of them to take off his neckcloth. "Put this around your face," he told her.

"What about you?"

He pulled the gag that was still tied around his head up around his mouth and nose. She nodded. "Mr. Jeffers, use your neckcloths to cover your mouths and noses," she said. She watched a moment while Jeffers did first his, then helped Lord Wheaten.

"Now, use the coal scuttle to move this coal behind us," she told Jeffers. She looked up again at the coal bin door. How were they going to reach it, and how were they going to get Lord Wheaten up there? She looked at Lord Wheaten, just standing there watching them. She brought the lantern to him. "Can you hold this up for Sir James?" Cecilia asked him.

"Hold for Sir James? Yes, I can hold for Sir James," he said happily.

Cecilia changed places with him and handed him the lantern. He held it up.

"Cecilia, what are you doing!" demanded James as he furiously dug at the coal.

"Getting a chair and some rope. We will need them when we reach the door." She skirted the pile of coal they'd piled into the servants' hall. She grabbed the rope she'd been tied with. It, at least, hadn't been cut. Then she dragged a chair toward the coal bin. She no longer needed a candle to light her way. The room was growing lighter, the air warmer and harder to breathe. They had little time left to make their escape.

She dragged the chair toward Jeffers, then took the coal scuttle from him. "Push the chair forward and have Lord Wheaten sit in it," she directed.

She bent to scoop the coal, then lifted the scuttle to throw the coal into the room behind them. She knew if the roof caved in, the coal would catch fire quickly and run back to the coal bin, but it couldn't be helped. They needed to put the coal someplace.

James passed the hearth shovel to Jeffers and went back to using his hands. Jeffers mimicked Cecilia's actions to move the coal behind them.

Cecilia's arms and her back ached, but she didn't stop until she felt James grab her arm.

"Enough!" he said. "See if you can get the door closed," he said, pointing to the low door to the servants' hall. "Having it closed now might earn us precious minutes. I'm going to try to open the bin door."

Despite their urgency, he gently encouraged Lord Wheaten to rise from the chair and placed it under the coal bin door. The door was heavy, but it wasn't locked as a London one would be. He bent his knees slightly, then pushed up with all his strength. The heavy door flew backward and smokey air streamed in.

He got down off the chair. "Jeffers, you first. You'll need to help Cecilia and Lord Wheaten."

Jeffers nodded and climbed the chair. Behind them, they heard a loud crash as the flames breached the servants' hall ceiling.

"I can't pull myself up!" Jeffers said. "I'm not strong enough."

"I'll boost you," said James. He put his head between the man's legs, then stood up, getting Jeffers to waist level with the ground above. He could pull himself out from there.

"Cecilia, you 're next," James ordered.

"No, let's get Lord Wheaten out. I think it will take the two of us to get him up and steady him so you can push him to Mr. Jeffers."

James didn't waste time arguing, they didn't have time to waste, instead he vowed silently they would not die here.

Cecilia got Lord Wheaten to the chair. "Can you bring your foot up to the chair?" Cecilia coaxed him. "Yes, hold on to the back. Now push up to stand on the chair. I'm going to help you." James lifted his other leg up while Cecilia steadied him. "James is going to lift you up now to Mr. Jeffers," she said, her arms up to steady Wheaten from listing to either side.

James lifted Wheaten as he had Jeffers and Mr. Jeffers pulled his weight off of James and out of the bin.

"Up you go, Cecilia," James said. He picked her up and set her on the chair, then grabbed her around her knees. "Be ready."

"Yes."

He tossed her up. She didn't land far enough out, but dangling.

"Jeffers!" James yelled as he pushed her legs up and she scrambled with her arms to pull herself out, her skirts tearing. James pushed her up a third time, and she was out.

Cecilia collapsed on the ground, getting her breath. "Jeffers!" she yelled, looking around for the man. She groaned. He was chasing after Lord Wheaten to keep him out of the fire. She looked down at James in the coal bin. "He's chasing after Lord Wheaten. Pass me the rope. There is a post here I can tie it around."

He handed the rope up to her. "The door behind me has started burning," he said as calmly as if he were speaking about the weather.

Cecilia tied the rope and hoped her knots were strong enough. She wanted to scream in frustration and curl up in a ball and cry, but that wouldn't help James. She sent the free end of the rope down to him. When she looked down, she saw some burning pieces of coal. He pulled himself up, but she could tell he was tired and his strength was waning.

"Come on, James, you can do it," she said urgently, her voice trembling.

He placed a hand higher on the rope and pulled his body up.

Suddenly James inched upward. Cecilia looked behind her to see Jeffers and Lord Wheaten straining to pull the rope up. Cecilia looked back at James as he reached out to grasp the edge of the coal bin frame. He used the momentum to get his leg and part of his foot up. With the two men pulling, he then got his knee up and pulled himself out of the bin. He rolled away from the edge.

Cecilia grabbed him, hugging him. The tears she'd

held back now leaving streaks down a coal-grimed face.

He pushed her back. "We have to get away from here," he said. "The coal is burning down there. The bin could collapse."

They help each other to their feet and staggered toward the stables. Jeffers and Lord Wheaten followed them. They turned back to look at the house as a great *whoosh* and crash collapsed the coal bin into a crater in the yard, sending up flames and sparks.

Two men and a boy ran around the corner of the barn, slowing only when they saw the extent of the conflagration. The flames shot up above the former roofline and roared as they devoured the house. Luckily the building was well away from other structures or trees, and the hollow where the house sat protected from all but the heaviest of winds. There would be no putting that fire out.

The boy spotted the Branstokes, Wheaten and Jeffers, and tugged on the oldest man's vest to get his attention. When the child pointed at them, the man looked over with a start. "Lord Wheaten, what happened?" said the man as he stared at their coal-streaked visages. "Are you alright?"

Lord Wheaten blinked at the man for a moment, then smiled. "We've had a fire, Mr. Willis!" Then he frowned. "I think they tried to kill us." He looked at his valet. "Jeffers, do you think they tried to kill us?"

"What? Who?" asked the man. He reached out toward Lord Wheaten.

"Yes, Lord Wheaten, I think they did," Jeffers said heavily.

Lord Wheaten nodded. He looked owlishly at the man. "I need to get to Folkestone. Tell the magistrate so I can get money for the veterans."

The men gaped at them, then they all turned to look at the burning building as another portion of the manor crashed.

"Mr. Jeffers," said James tiredly, "please take Lord Wheaten into the stables out of the sun and see if you can get him to rest."

"Yes, Sir James," he said, leading his employer into the barn.

James watched them go, then turned back to the strangers. "I am Sir James Branstoke, and this is my wife, Lady Branstoke."

"Tom Willis," the man said, bobbing his head forward. "This here is my brother, George Willis and my son, David Willis. We're from the home farm. We saw the smoke, so that's how we came to be here. What happened? Lord Wheaten said something about someone trying to kill you?"

"Yes. We were bound in the servants' hall with Lord Wheaten and his man by men who stole government property and hid it in this stable." James stared at the stables for a moment, his hands on his hips. Cecilia came up behind him to lay her hand on his back. He looked down at her. She'd truly awed him this day, this slip of a woman with the courage of a lion. He'd told Soothcoor right. His wife was rarer than gold. He pulled her to his side and dropped a kiss on her forehead, heedless of the strangers before them. Unfortunately, the day wasn't over yet. There was much to be done. The men had gone from thieves to would-be murderers. Cecilia could have died. Bloody hell, they all could have died if not for Cecilia's weak female ruse.

He wondered why men were so quick to believe women weak. Today, he would be grateful for the general belief. He knew he shouldn't encourage Cecilia's deceptive behavior; however, if men were going to be blind to his wife's intelligent subterfuge, that was not his concern.

James looked back at Tom Willis. "How far away are we from Dover?"

"Not more'n five miles."

"We need to get there as soon as possible. Do you know Mrs. Yates?"

The man grinned. "Everyone between Folkestone and Dover knows Mrs. Yates."

"We need to get to Mrs. Yates' cottage as soon as possible," James said.

Mr. Willis turned toward his brother. "George, harness up the wagon and fetch Mum and her basket of herbs for Lord Wheaten."

"I'll fetch the horse from the field," the boy, David, said, and turned to run back the way they'd come as George trotted off toward their farm.

MRS. WILLIS TOOK one look at Cecilia and James and she started shouting orders at her menfolk. Fetch water, towel, a comb, Mr. Willis' old coat, the slouch hat he wore when he worked in the fields, her red cloak, a straw hat, and a scarf, were among her orders.

She set Mr. Jeffers to grinding some herbs together in a small mortar with a pestle she'd pulled out of her basket to make a tisane for Lord Wheaten while she attended the Branstokes. After they washed away coal dust from their face, neck, and hands, she directed James to don her husband's old coat and slouch hat, and for Cecilia to put on her red cloak and straw hat with a scarf tied over the top of it to keep it on her head and to further disguise her.

There was nothing they could do for their soiled and ripped clothing; however, that did not concern anyone. James grew impatient to be off, but only Cecilia recognized his impatience—outwardly he remained the calm gentleman. She wondered how others could not see his agitation. Then she realized she saw it in his eyes. The more hooded his gaze became, the greater his impatience. He hid his emotions by hiding his eyes.

18

I t was late afternoon before they pulled the wagon up to Mrs. Yates' cottage.

Cecilia climbed down from the wagon seat, but before she could knock on the door, Mrs. Yates bustled out.

"Praise be, yur here! We have a right ruckus!" she said, clutching her apron in her hands. Her eyes widened when she looked at them. "What happened to ye?"

Cecilia laughed at Mrs. Yates' abrupt change in manner. Though she hadn't had access to a mirror, she knew by looking at James, and down at her own clothes, that she and James looked like citizens of the Seven Dials slum district of London. She longed for a bath, but that luxury would not be possible for hours to come. "We will tell you all. But where might James take the wagon?" Cecilia asked.

"Oh!" Mrs. Yates said, dragging her eyes away from their dirty and ripped clothes. "Reuben. Reuben be here. He can take the wagon." She opened the door. "Reuben!" she called. John Coachman came to the door. In the background came a noise of muffled screeches and wood hitting stone. "Sir James! Lady Branstoke!" he cried out in relief.

"Reuben, take the wagon to The Hound and Hare, then come back quick as a bunny," directed Mrs. Yates.

James and John Coachman changed places on the wagon seat. James clapped John Coachman on the shoulder as they passed each other.

"In, in, quick like," Mrs. Yates said. She looked down the lane in both directions to see who might be about.

Inside the cottage, Cecilia and James were confronted with Captain Melville, bound and gagged in the chair Cecilia had sat in the previous evening. His eyes wide, Melville tried to communicate with them through his gag, bumping his chair toward them to get them to untie him. James looked over at Aldrich. Aldrich was dressed and lying on top of the bedclothes. His color had improved. He looked like a lounging gentleman instead of a man recovering from a knife wound. Elinor sat on the edge of the bed. The fingers of her right hand entwined with those of her husband.

"Melville doesn't believe Captain Dunnett is involved in the subsidy theft," Aldrich explained. "He wanted to fetch Dunnett here. Your coachman had to convince him otherwise."

"And the gag?" James asked, biting back a laugh.

"The gag is because he yelled his fool head off. We had to shut him up."

James looked back at Melville. "Captain, I take it you have not received any recent communications from Candelstone," he stated. "If you had, you would know Captain Dunnett is up to his eyeballs in this mess." Exasperated at the man's mule-headedness, he unwrapped the bandages Mrs. Willis had put on his wrists. "See these rope marks on my wrists? Dunnett's handiwork." The raw, angry red and bloody skin looked like someone tried to sever his hands from his wrists.

Confusion twisted Melville's features, and the color drained from his cheeks as he stared at James' wrists.

Mrs. Yates clucked her tongue. "Let me get you salve for them rope burns," she said. "And we'll get them bandaged back up." She scurried over to a ceramic jar on the mantel.

Cecilia took off her cloak and hat and laid them on the table. Elinor gasped at the state of Cecilia's clothes. Her dress, once a light peach ornamented with cream lace, was dusted with soot and streaked with black. A strip of lace from her bodice hung loose, a corner tear at knee height revealed her chemise underneath and her pale blond hair now looked powdered gray from coal soot.

"What happened?" Aldrich asked.

"We were driving to Folkestone to see Mr. Pollock when four men blocked our way," James said, removing the slouch hat and Mr. Willis' oversized coat. He looked nearly as bad as Cecilia. His clothes little more than rags. Only the cut of his boots—though they, too, were filthy and scraped—could indicate his means.

"Though I now wonder if that would have been a futile errand if we had made it to Folkestone. One of the men I recognized was Pollock's butler," James continued.

"Who was that?" Aldrich asked.

"Pollock addressed him as Bernard, so I assumed he is Bernard Oakes."

"Big man, hair shorn, beetle-browed, looks like he should be a pugilist?" Aldrich asked.

"Yes."

"That's Oakes. And you say he was acting as the butler at Pollock's estate?"

"Yes. He was the servant Pollock sent to fetch the portmanteau to give to me."

Aldrich frowned. "That is worrisome news. We didn't think Pollock was that deep into this mess. We knew the smugglers resented the subsidy theft activities as dragging too much attention to the area and their activity but we didn't think they would completely join with them." Aldrich swung his legs around to sit on the edge of the bed. Elinor tried to stop him, but he shook his head. "And I didn't know Oakes associated with Pollock and the smugglers."

Mrs. Yates came up to James and pushed his sleeve back so she could put salve and clean bandages on his wrists. "There be a passel of Oakes in these parts," she said. "I myself knows three named Bernard—cousins all named after their granddaddy. All the Oakes be a fighting bunch just fer the fun of it." She looked up at James. "Ye would think they were Irish!" she said with a cackle. She finished rubbing in the salve on one wrist and reached for his other wrist.

"Well that knowledge doesn't help us determine if Pollock is associated with Yarnell and Dunnett or not," groused Aldrich.

"Maybe, maybe not, but Mr. Pollock, he come from a line of free traders in the area and his wife, she's from those plying the Cornish coast. They has a certain pride, if you know what I mean. The Oakes, now them be opportunists through and through."

"And yet he's the magistrate," James mused.

"And a good one, too, so long as the matter don't

involve smuggling, leastways the smuggling he be party to. —I just had thought," Mrs. Yates said, wiping her fingers on her apron. "Did the Bernard ye seen at Mr. Pollock's have a scar on his chin?" she asked, tracing a half-moon shape on her chin.

James shook his head. "Not that I recall."

"The Bernard Oakes that I knew with Yarnell and Dunnett has one," Aldrich said.

Mrs. Yates nodded. "Cousins. Not the same man," she said as she unrolled a length of clean cloth to put around his wrists.

Both men nodded, thinking about the implications for there being Oakes cousins.

"Because of my uncertainty about Pollock, I was going to send John Coachman to London to let Candelstone know what is happening, but given the attempted murder today, things are happening too fast and that's too far away to have any chance of Candelstone rendering assistance," James said.

"Might be best to communicate to Candelstone through military channels," Aldrich suggested.

Captain Melville thumped his chair toward them and tried to speak through the gag. They ignored him.

"What are you thinking?" James asked Aldrich.

"This Sergeant Major Kendall that Mrs. Yates has sent for, he can arrange messaging and get through the London bureaucratic hierarchy best, too."

"So we can send John Coachman for Pollock," James said.

"Exactly my thoughts. Who were the other men involved this afternoon?" Aldrich asked.

"Bishop Yarnell, who appeared to be the leader, Captain Dunnett, and Stephen, a young man Cecilia says is employed by Mr. Tinsley."

"Stephen!" said Mrs. Yates. "Oh, no," she said as she collapsed down on her chair.

"You know him?" Cecilia asked.

"Aye, good lad, how did he get to be with them, I'm wonderin'?"

"I think he didn't realize what he was getting into. At least when he tied me up, he tied me up loosely. If he hadn't, we wouldn't be here now," Cecilia said.

Mrs. Yates nodded, but Cecilia saw a tear slide down her cheek.

"What happened?" Aldrich asked.

Cecilia swallowed. "After they bound us, they set the house on fire," she said baldly.

"Yarnell had decided that the fact I have been seen with Candelstone recently, and that I am not on my honeymoon in the highlands, as we put about, means I am obviously one of Candelstone's spies," James said disgustedly.

"And because of that, Yarnell decided to get rid of you permanently," Aldrich said. He rubbed his hands down his face.

"It is only because that young man tied Cecilia loosely that we are here now," James explained. "She was able to untie her ropes, then free the rest of us."

"Us?" Aldrich asked.

"Lord Jasper Wheaten and his valet, Mr. Jeffers, were also tied up. They had us in the servants' hall below stairs at Woodhaven Manor."

Aldrich nodded. "It was only a matter of time before they turned on Wheaten," he said.

"Lord Wheaten is not well," Cecilia said. "Mr. Jeffers said he has suffered several apoplectic fits as of late."

Melville thumped his chair again. This time they

looked at him. He again made the inarticulate sounds behind his gag, his pitch higher and more strident.

"Are you going to yell again?" Aldrich asked him.

He shook his head no. James came up behind him to remove his gag.

"Thank you," Melville said. Then, when James stepped away, he frowned. "Aren't you going to untie me, too?"

"No. As I told you several days ago at Bartlett Hall, I don't trust you, and since then you have continued to prove my distrust is warranted."

John Coachman opened the door to the cottage. A tall man in uniform followed him in.

"Sergeant Major!" Mrs. Yates said, her face lit with delight. "I see ye got me message. We need yur help," she said eagerly. She took him by the arm to bring him forward. The military man was taller than John Coachman and older, his brown hair liberally salted with gray. Standing next to him, Mrs. Yates looked like one of her dolls.

"Lord Aldrich, Sir James, this here be Sergeant Major Kendall, who I told ye about. He's the one who can help us."

"Hello, Mr. Kendall. Thank you for coming," James said. "This is Lord and Lady Aldrich. I am Sir James Branstoke, and this is my wife, Lady Branstoke."

"Private Yates and I were with Sir James in Spain," Mrs. Yates explained.

The Sergeant Major saluted Sir James.

James shook his head. "I am no longer with the military, Sergeant Kendall. However, Lord Aldrich here is with the foreign office."

"Mr. Kendall!" barked Melville. "I order you to untie me at once!" Though tied to the chair, he lifted his chin high to look down his nose at the soldier, his lips pursed together.

Kendall looked at Melville, then raised an eyebrow in inquiry to Mrs. Yates.

Mrs. Yates clucked her tongue as she shook her head. "He says he's a captain, but I don't know. Looks too young to me and I ain't seen proof," she said as she teetered back to her chair by the fire.

"This is an outrage! Sir James! Lord Aldrich! I demand you tell him who I am!" Melville said.

James and Lord Aldrich exchanged glances. Aldrich shrugged.

"I'll tell you," Cecilia said, stepping forward, her hands on her slim hips.

"Thank you, my lady," crowed Melville, glaring at James and Lord Aldrich.

"He's the nodcock who hired a man to break into my room at The Seagull in the middle of the night to frighten Lady Aldrich and me," Cecilia said. "And the next morning he had the effrontery to steal a letter right out of my hand and would have gotten away with it if it hadn't been for my husband, Sir James."

"What?! No!" protested Captain Melville.

"Are you calling me a liar?" Cecilia countered, glaring at him.

"No, but—"

"Be quiet, Melville, or we'll put the gag back on you," Lord Aldrich said as he stood up. He grabbed his side and winced slightly as he straightened. Elinor looked sad and worried.

"What is this all about? Did this man have anything to do with the state of your clothing?" Kendall asked.

"No, but a Captain Dunnett, who I understand is stationed here in Dover, did," Cecilia said.

"Dunnett!" Kendall exclaimed, looking from one face to another.

Lord Aldrich sat back down on the edge of the bed. "You are aware, Mr. Kendall, of the subsidies England sends to our allies for their support in the war against Napoleon?" he asked.

"Yes, my lord. My battalion did security duty with a couple shipments last year."

"There have been additional shipments this year, smaller, scattered shipments as there have been conspiracies to steal them. Spreading out the shipments was deemed an efficient way to minimize the risk. I found out about a plan to steal one of the shipments, but instead of a shipment of all money, this shipment also included the latest in English weaponry and ammunition. Unfortunately, we could not prevent the theft. We were under orders to let the theft occur so we could capture all participants together. An admirable idea in theory; however, it did not work out that way in practice."

"A Candelstone theory," Elinor said in quiet disgust. "The only kind he has."

Aldrich looked at his wife and nodded. "And I should have recalled of his pattern before I agreed with the plan."

He turned back to the soldier. "The plan now is to recover the gold and weapons before the gold lines their pockets and the weapons disappear out of the country. We know that at one time the stolen goods were at Woodhaven Manor, but they were recently moved from there to, we believe, the Western Heights, to one of the abandoned tunnel projects."

Sergeant Major Kendall nodded. "Closer to water," he observed.

"Yes. We think the thieves intend the armament for Napoleon," said James.

Kendall's dark eyebrows snapped together. "We'll not let that happen!" he decreed.

"I was trusting you to feel that way," Aldrich said with a wry smile.

James crossed his arms over his chest. "This morning, Lady Branstoke and I saw what we think is part of the shipment in the stables at Woodhaven. Less than an hour later, that stable was empty. From the discussion we overheard, because of the weight and bulkiness of the gold and the weapons, we surmise, they had to move the goods in stages, and what remained in the barn before today was for the last shipment. They have some location between the Heights and Woodhaven where they temporarily stow the wagon and rest the draft horses before moving toward the tunnels and caves. What they stole is heavy and bulky. They have had to move it a bit at a time so they wouldn't draw attention to their actions. I imagine what they moved from Woodhaven is resting now in this middle location and will be moved tonight to the Western Heights tunnels."

"How familiar are you, Mr. Kendall, with the unused parts of the Western Heights?" Aldrich asked.

"Not well, myself; however, I have a couple of privates that I know have been all over that area. But I wouldn't think we need to know about all the unfinished tunnels. If they are moving goods tonight, we can stake out the area to find what direction they go and follow them," Kendall suggested.

Aldrich nodded. "True, but if we know where to go ahead of time, that could ensure we don't miss them."

Kendall nodded as he thought. "Private Mead roams the hills all around Dover whenever he can. He

will know the best areas to be on the watch," Kendall
offered.

"Can you trust him?" Aldrich asked. "Gold can be
a powerful incentive to steal."

Sergeant Major Kendall turned his head to Mrs.
Yates. "What do you think, Maggie, can we trust
Mead?"

Mrs. Yates scratched her chin. "Aye, I think so.
Can ye bring him here to meet the gentlemen? I
know if young Mead were to see Lady Branstoke's
ripped and dirty clothin', he'd be rarin' to bring
mischief to the thieves. He don't brook no disrespect
to women and hims a banty cock if he hears of
any."

Cecilia looked down at her ruined gown and
laughed. "I never thought my new look would be a
benefit."

"I'll get some of my men together. Most should be
at barracks. We're preparing to ship out to join
Wellington's army day after tomorrow. Maggie, looks
like you got a passel of mouths to feed afore tonight.
I'll have my Sally bring some food to ya."

"Let me pay you," Aldrich said, reaching for his
money pouch.

"No, sir, 'tain't necessary," the Sergeant Major said,
drawing himself up tall. "Maggie, thank you for
bringing this to my attention. This is just what the
boys and I need to get us prepared to fight Napoleon,
sharpen our wits."

"We have one more request before you leave, Sergeant Major," said Aldrich.

"Yes, sir?"

"We need you to send a man to London as soon as
possible to deliver a message to Lord Candelstone
about this situation. We need someone who will be

diligent to see it gets into Candelstone's hand and no other. He can't be fobbed off."

"I understand, Lord Aldrich."

"Mrs. Yates," Aldrich said, "do you have paper and something to write with? I don't care if all you have is charcoal."

Mrs. Yates laughed. "Aye, I can do better than that." She went to a bureau to pull out paper and pencil and brought them to Lord Aldrich.

Quickly, Aldrich wrote his message to Lord Candelstone, then handed it to the officer.

Sergeant Major Kendall took the paper, saluted Lord Aldrich and Sir James, then left.

"Mrs. Yates," James said, "I was wondering if you would you have any idea where the wagons could be hidden before taken to the Western Heights?"

"I been thinkin' on that," she said. She got up from her chair to stoke the fire. "Mr. Tinsley, he has another stable and pasture, a bit away. That's where he keeps more horses fer his coachin' inn. It be also where they say smugglers often lay their goods afore sellin' 'em. I figure if young Stephen's workin' with them thieves, it's 'cause Tinsley told him to." She ladled water from a barrel into a kettle and hung it on the hob.

James looked at Aldrich. "Tinsley mentioned another stable. Said that was where the horses involved in the carriage accident were. I've been suspicious of Tinsley's involvement," he said, "Melville?"

"Yes?" he answered sulkily.

"Did you get Tinsley to agree to allow that man to sneak into Lady Branstoke and Lady Aldrich's room that night?"

"Get him to agree, it was his idea," he groused. "Didn't do me a lot of good."

"What?!" Cecilia and Elinor exclaimed together.

"What do you mean it was Tinsley's idea?" Cecilia demanded. Her fair brows drew together. "What brought it up as an idea in the first place?"

"I told him I needed to speak with Lady Aldrich, that it was important government business, but you and Sir James wouldn't let me. He's the one who suggested giving you a bit of a scare, to make you more amenable to speaking with me," he told Elinor. "And it was one of his men who actually came into your room."

"Do you know if the idea always was for him to go out the window?" Cecilia asked.

"Yes, it was."

"Which is probably why you couldn't find him, John Coachman, when you went after him. He didn't have to run away, just hide on the property," Cecilia said to their coachman.

"Yes, milady, for that had me stumped as to how he was gone so fast. But you don't need to call me John Coachman anymore. Nor you, Sir James," he said, looking over at him. "You can call me Reuben."

"Oh! And why is that?" Cecilia asked.

"I been talkin' to Mrs. Yates," he said slowly. He scratched his head. "I got nothin' to be ashamed or embarrassed about the military. I saw good service afore I were shot. Them ghosts can be laid ter rest as we all got 'em. I'm not gonna deny from my past. I am Sir James' John Coachman. That's just my job. I am Reuben Uttley."

Cecilia smiled and walked up to hold her hand out to him. "I'm pleased to meet you, Mr. Uttley," she said.

He looked at her hand a moment, and then a big grin spread across his broad face and he shook her hand.

James came up and slapped him on the back. "You

are a good man, and I'll address you however you want to be addressed, even if you say you're King George."

Reuben laughed, and the tension in his shoulders eased.

James turned back to Melville. "I'm curious. What else did you tell Tinsley? Did you tell him about the stolen subsidies?"

"Yes," Melville admitted, not meeting James' gaze.

"But you wouldn't tell us," James said.

Melville flushed. "I've been a nodcock, like Lady Branstoke said."

"That would be an appropriate descriptive word," Aldrich agreed.

"Let me redeem myself!" he said eagerly.

"And how do you propose to do that?" Aldrich asked.

"Let me go with you tonight."

Lord Aldrich looked at James.

James shrugged. "That is for you to decide, as you both work for Candelstone."

Aldrich compressed his lips for a moment. "All right, but only because I believe that is what Candelstone would expect."

James looked over at Reuben Uttley and motioned him toward Melville. "John—I mean Reuben, would you untie the captain, please? If Captain Melville will be accompanying us, I have another task for you."

"Yes, sir," Reuben said, though he didn't look happy with the task of freeing Melville. The big man pulled a knife out of his boot, then squatted down behind Melville to cut the ropes.

Melville stood up to shake his legs out and stretch his arms, then he sat back down again. "Now, we need to make our plan. As Lord Aldrich is injured, I am the ranking officer with the foreign office and—"

"Melville, be quiet and get out of that chair!" James said with biting precision.

Cecilia laughed, then covered her mouth guiltily. Melville was at least consistent in his bombastic manner. She did not envy James handling this man.

"But we have to plan," protested Melville. "I have paper and pencil in my pocket somewhere," he said, patting his pockets to find the items.

"Melville!" James roared.

Melville looked up. "Yes, Sir James? I was—"

"I know what you are doing and what you are not doing. I told you to be quiet and to get up *OUT OF THAT CHAIR!* Now! Or I will request Mr. Uttley to bodily remove you from said chair and toss you in the corner!"

Melville jumped to his feet.

James pulled the chair back away from him, then turned to Cecilia. "My dear, please sit down," he said calmly.

Elinor giggled from her perch on the bed. Lord Aldrich smirked.

"And now, Captain Melville, let's get one thing perfectly clear. You will plan nothing. You will take orders like the rest of Sergeant Major Kendall's men. Until we have finished tonight, consider yourself demoted."

"You can't do that!" he protested.

"No, Sir James can't, but I can," said Lord Aldrich. "Your lack of judgement throughout this affair is appalling. Your father should never have purchased a captaincy for you, and so I shall tell him unless you can redeem yourself in the next several hours, which, given your behavior this afternoon, I find highly suspect. You will be quiet and take orders. Do I make my-self clear?"

"But—" Melville tried.

Lord Aldrich shook his head. "No."

Melville turned to storm out the door. When he grabbed the door handle and opened it, James slammed it shut again. "You don't want to do that. You are known to the thieves. You need to stay here and wait with us for Mr. Kendall. If you want to redeem yourself, you need to take orders."

He sat, sulking, on the edge of the table. James and Lord Aldrich exchanged exasperated looks.

James turned to his coachman. "Reuben, Lord Aldrich and I were talking earlier. We need you to go to Folkestone to get Mr. Pollock. Maybe Lord Wheaten and Jeffers have gone on to Folkestone, but I wouldn't place a wager on that given Wheaten's health. Rent a good, swift horse from The Hound and Hare. Hope-fully, you can get there before full-on dark. Tell Pol-lock what has happened today. I'd write a letter but I think it will be quicker if you speak to him. Tell him we believe the gold and weapons are in the Western Heights and we are going after them tonight."

Reuben almost saluted before he caught himself. "Yes, Sir James," he said. He opened the door and left.

Mrs. Yates rose from her chair. "Lady Aldrich, Lady Branstoke, water's boiling. Would ye care for tea?"

19

M rs. Kendall brought bread, stew, and meat pies. Cecilia was concerned for the largess shown by the Kendalls and made a promise to herself that she would see the Kendalls repaid in one way or another.

Sergeant Major Kendall and Private Mead came and went as they were eating. Private Mead's eyes gleamed with excitement when told of the situation, the more so when told they would take Captain Dunnett prisoner. He was not a popular officer.

Kendall said he would return at full dark.

"I'm going with you," Aldrich said.

"Simon, no!" protested Elinor.

Aldrich grabbed both her hands in his. "I must go, my sweet. This is my mission. My last mission."

"Lord Aldrich, I have seen you wince when you move," James said. "You are not in any condition—"

"I will be fine," Aldrich said, cutting him off. "We do what we must," he said, staring at James. "I'm sure those wrists hurt like bloody hell, too."

James studied the man, then nodded.

"If'n yur goin' to go, best let me bind ye tighter," Mrs. Yates said. She pulled a length of brown fabric from a shelf and tore it with her teeth to get a rip started, then pulled the fabric apart to get long bands.

"That's a new piece of cloth!" Cecilia said.

"Aye, was plannin' on a new skirt, but there be others," Mrs. Yates said calmly. "This is clean and be the right width now fer a binding. Now, Lord Aldrich, if ye would remove yur waistcoat and shirt, we'll get ye bound up good.

"Now, miladies," she said as she worked, "I know ye be frettin' and would go with yur men, but men as it goin' into battle can't be havin' their minds distracted worrin' about ye. Ye stay here right and tight with me and they be back quick as a bunny. Ye be seein'. From what I heard tell, ye both done good, comin' ter their rescue. Time to let them fight the big battle.

"Now milord, how does that feel? Can ye breath still?" Mrs. Yates asked with a cackle.

"Yes, and that makes it feel better. Thank you," Aldrich said.

"Lady Aldrich," Mrs. Yates said, "Yur goin' to need to help him get his shirt and waistcoat back on." She picked up his shirt from the bed and handed it to Elinor, and then she turned toward Cecilia. "Yur lion hearted, milady. For yur a wee thing I make no mistake about that, but best ye lie down with us sheep right now," she said, giving her a side-eyed knowing look.

Cecilia did not know what to say. Yes, she had been bound to go with the men, thinking of refusing to be left behind, but if she did, so would Elinor and there would be two men, two leaders, with their attentions divided, for Cecilia was not naïve enough to think James or Aldrich could pursue the thieves without thinking on her and Elinor's safety. They were not those kinds of men, for which she and Elinor were fortunate. She would have to stay behind, for all it would chafe her. But if they weren't returned by morning, she would go on the hunt herself. That was a promise she would make to herself!

James put his arm about his wife's shoulders. "Thank you, Mrs. Yates, for making the argument I couldn't."

"I followed the drum fer too many years. I know fer what I say," she said tiredly. She put a hand on the small of her back as she straightened and picked up her supplies, then walked back to her chair by the fireplace.

When Kendall returned, Cecilia and Elinor sat together on the edge of the bed. They weren't happy, but they would not importune their husbands. But they held each other's hands as they watched Aldrich, James, and Melville follow Sergeant Major Kendall into the night.

THE MEN FOLLOWED the Sergeant Major as he led them down noisome back streets and alleyways west to the outskirts of town. A three-quarter moon in a cloudless sky provided just enough light to proceed steadily.

They scrambled down a small hillside to a thicket of trees where a handful of Kendall's soldiers waited with a wagon, several men holding unlit torches along with their weapons.

"We found it! We found a cavern with crates with government stamps on them!" exclaimed Private Mead, running up to them.

"Sh-sh," warned Kendall. "Sound travels in the night air. Best you remember that now."

Private Mead ducked his head in contrition. "Yes, sir," he said.

James clapped him on the shoulder. "Now, Private, tell us what you found," he whispered.

Everyone gathered close to hear the private.

"It were easy, if you were out here lookin'. They musta pulled a load here after the last rain. There's grass trampled and deep ruts in the earth. Whatever they brought here must be heavy. The tracks led almost directly to an old tunnel entrance. A big bush hid it, but it weren't hard to find. This way, sir."

Private Mead led the way. They walked only about half a mile before they stopped to point at the ruts in the ground.

"Careful, these ruts make for hard walking."

Ahead were several large bushes and some straggly trees fighting for space on the hillside. The privates walked to the left and pointed ahead of them. It surprised James to see the darkness behind the bush was not more bushes, but an archway, the front edge of which was lined with brick.

"Where are we?" James whispered to Mr. Kendall.

"Just south of the detached bastion," Mr. Kendall said.

"Bastion?"

"It's to protect our flank. Most of the gun emplacements face the sea to guard against an attack by Napoleon from the sea."

"But after the Battle of Trafalgar, Napoleon's navy was decimated."

"Yes, sir, but we need to protect our weakest point, regardless. The fort is an amazing defensive structure for the country. Barracks for three thousand men, storage for guns and explosives, everything designed to take an explosive hit that would not affect another area," Kendal explained.

"Some years ago, it was determined that the back side of the Western Heights is vulnerable to attack, so they started fortifications here in 1804 to protect the backside. That is where we are going."

"Amazing!" James said.

"To your left, up the hill, is the north detached bastion. There are four-gun emplacements there along with magazines. It is surrounded by a ten-foot-tall dry moat. It is not finished, yet; work slowed after Trafalgar when it looked like Napoleon would no longer be able to invade Britain, and stopped when he was captured. The tunnel, or magazine, or gun emplacement we will go into looks to be one that was built earlier, but had work stopped on it in favor of work on the bastion with its higher elevation."

Sergeant Major Kendall directed most of the men to fan out along the hillside and stand watch as they went in. He instructed one man to fetch the wagon and bring it as close to this location as they could, but keep it hidden in the cut ravines that marred the hillside. He lit his torch from flint and tinder in his pouch, then lit Private Mead's torch.

"Lead on, Mead," he said.

"They didn't go far in, sir. Just into this next room to the right," Mead said as he eagerly led them forward.

Inside the approximately one hundred forty-foot square brick-lined room were stacks of crates of varying sizes and shapes.

James stared at the stacks, amazed at the quantity. "How did they manage to steal this much without getting caught? This has to be the work of more than those we know are involved."

He walked over to the crates. Someone had pried the top of one crate up. Inside were the new model Baker rifles. He pulled one out and passed it to Sergeant Major Kendall to see, then peered into other crates.

"That is government property, Sir James," protested Captain Melville, moving forward to grab the rifle out of the sergeant major's hands. "We need to confiscate this and return it to the government immediately. I will go get the rest of the men to help—"

"You will do no such thing, Captain. May I remind you I told you, you are to follow orders here. You are not in charge," Aldrich said. "Return the rifle to Sergeant Major Kendall."

"I doubt we could move all of this quickly with the number of men we have. Some of these crates are overly heavy and this one here," James said, pointing to one leaning upward against three other crates, "shows signs of the crate breaking apart."

"What is all this?" Private Mead asked.

"These are goods and gold our government is sending to our allies," Aldrich said.

"Gold?" Private Mead repeated in a hushed voice.

"See those smaller square boxes over there? Try to pick one up," suggested Aldrich.

"Don't touch it!" yelled Captain Melville.

"Melville!" warned Aldrich.

Private Mead looked at his commanding officer. Kendall indicated with a wave of his hand to go ahead.

Mead tried to lift the crate. He only managed a couple of inches before he had to put it down. "It would take two men to carry each one of these!"

"Exactly," Aldrich said.

"Instead of removing them, I wonder if we can

move them elsewhere," James said. "Do you know if there are other rooms like this?"

"Yes, sir, though not all as dug out as much as this one. And this tunnel is like others that have been dug out. They have similar layouts. This way, sir."

He led them to a branching room to the left, and one further on, branching to the right. At the end of the tunnel another room was started, but full of rubble.

"This is where the built tunnel ends. I think there was to be stairs to connect to another tunnel that way," he said, pointing up and to the left. "See, you can see the other tunnel from here. Just a mound of rubble to get there right now, but they do connect."

"I wonder if our thieves are aware of this connection."

"I'd say not, sir. No one has been this way."

"Thank you, Private. I noted the second room we went in was full of bricks for the revetment, but the corridor walls, ceiling, and floor have not been done yet," James said.

"I wager that be fer staging purposes, sir."

James nodded. "Hmm, yes, that would make sense."

"Sir James, since it looks like the bricks are staged, why don't we stage the gold crates in the other rooms? If they are not here, Yarnell and the others will probably reach the conclusion someone has stolen them," Aldrich suggested.

"Excellent suggestion. And Mr. Kendall, if it is all right with you, I'd like to have Private Mead see if he can get to the next tunnel. We may need a back door."

"Aye, that is sound thinking, Sir James. Private Mead, you up for scrambling that rubble field to the next tunnel?"

"Yes, sir!" he said.

"Off you go, then," Kendall said. He turned to James and Aldrich. "I'm going to collect a couple of my soldiers to help carry this lot."

"Aldrich, you are in no shape to carry any of these, but I'd ask if you can carry a torch for us," James said.

"Yes, I can do that," Aldrich said.

"Melville, you're with me," James said as he shrugged out of his coat. He rolled up his sleeves.

"You expect me to carry crates?" Melville asked.

"Yes, I do. With me. Come, let's get started. I'm not waiting on Kendall and his men."

"But we don't do manual labor," Melville protested.

James planted his hands on his hips and glared at Melville. "It never stops with you, does it? I do manual labor and you will as well, or I'll request Mr. Kendall to use his bayonet on your buttocks to give you a reason you can't help."

"Just say the word, Sir James," Kendall said jovially as he strode back into the tunnel with three of his men. He leveled his rifle bayonet at Captain Melville's backside.

"And we will all swear it was an accident," said Aldrich.

"All right!" Melville said. He followed James to a crate and picked up his end, though he grumbled at the weight and claimed they were going to injure their backs. James and the other men ignored him.

Working together, the soldiers, James and Captain Melville made quick work of the gold crates, and when they were done, Aldrich took off his jacket and used the bottom hem to dust away their footprints to the back room.

"Now, let's take the weapons and ammunition out of here," Aldrich said.

"What do we do about the busted crate?" one soldier asked.

"Leave it. The thieves will know they are in the right place and that someone has stolen their prize," the Sergeant Major said.

Aldrich grinned. "Let's make it more obvious."

"What are you suggesting?" James asked.

"Let's let them know we have the weapons. Ahh— Captain Melville! We have a task for you," Aldrich said. "A redemption task, if you can handle it."

"What?"

"Take the wagon and a few men and get the weapons back to the barracks. We can't let Yarnell and Dunnett sell them to the French!"

"No!"

Aldrich frowned. "No, you won't command the wagon or no, you won't stop Yarnell and Dunnett?"

"No! I mean, yes, I will do this and no, I won't let the weapons go to Napoleon," he grumbled.

"Good, then as Sergeant Major Kendall would say, off you go, then."

James and Aldrich watched Captain Melville issue commands to four soldiers outside to accompany him on his mission. He ordered them in formation behind the wagon.

"What is he doing?" Aldrich asked.

James dolefully shook his head. "He's playing soldiers. We will definitely have to ensure he sells out."

"He's likely to get them killed," Sergeant Major Kendall growled. He trotted out to the wagon and his soldiers.

James and Aldrich couldn't hear what they said, but they could tell Captain Melville was unhappy. One man climbed into the wagon with Melville and the driver. The rest of the soldiers came back and took positions in the scrub thickets around the tunnel entrance.

The wagon lurched slowly forward. Even with only the crates of weapons in the wagon, the load was precariously heavy. Would the wagon make it back to the barracks, or would the thieves discover them on the way? It was a gamble either way.

"I hope Yarnell and company see the wagon and split up," James said. He turned to face Aldrich. "They've got to know not all the stolen goods can be in one wagon."

Aldrich nodded. "It would help if some go after the wagon and the others continue on to the tunnel for the gold. I would think it depends on their level of greed."

"I'm thinking Captain Dunnett will go after the weapons. He knows their value, and they're easier for him to transport and sell," Sergeant Major Kendall said. "I suggested to Captain Melville that if the thieves come after them, they're to surrender the weapons. He protested, but my men understood. Best I could do with that one."

"If the two soldiers run, Melville won't stay to fight," James said. "He's not like his sister."

Aldrich laughed. "No one is like Lady Isabella Blessingame."

"No one except for my wife," James said softly, smiling.

20

C ecilia sipped her tea and waited thirty minutes.

Mrs. Yates was correct; James would worry if she were with him. What he failed to realize is the amount of her worry with him out of her sight. He was going into a dangerous situation against men who had no compunction to murder. A little backup help, a surprise to everyone, might be the deciding factor in success against these men. And she had read the papers of women who followed the drum and loaded spare muskets and even picked up the guns of fallen men, taken their places in the lines, and manned cannons.

"Mrs. Yates, do you know the rendezvous spot Sargent Major Kendall spoke of?"

Mrs. Yates looked up from her stitching. Her head canted to the side as she considered Cecilia's question. "Yes, milady, I do," she said, a sly smile curving up her lips.

"Then you can guide me there."

"Aye," she answered slowly.

"Cecilia! What are you thinking?" asked Elinor.

Cecilia turned to Elinor. "I'm thinking we should follow the drum."

Mrs. Yates' cackling laughter filled her small cottage. "Yur a plucky one. Do ye have any weapons?"

Cecilia sighed deeply. "No, I do not."

"I have a knife," Elinor said.

"A knife?" Cecilia asked. "Where did you get it? What kind of knife?"

"Aisha gave it to me. She said they call it a *katar*." Elinor lifted her skirt to show the knife and sheath buckled to her leg. It did not have a vertical handle, but a horizontal handle attached to side prongs that ran up either side of the handle.

"Do either of ye know how to shoot?" Mrs. Yates asked.

"I do," Cecilia said. "My grandfather taught me."

"Your grandfather?" Elinor asked.

Cecilia laughed. "Yes. My grandfather has an interesting past. He was once a highwayman."

"But I thought your grandfather was a duke, or was that the other one?"

"No, my grandfather, the Duke of Houghton, was once a highwayman. It made my mother and grandmother angry, but he taught me to shoot. Pistol and musket. I haven't tried a rifle yet," she said.

"And what about loading yur weapon?"

"Of course. My grandfather insisted on it."

Mrs. Yates nodded. "Good. And ye, Lady Aldrich?" she asked.

"No, I'm afraid not."

"No matter. I only have one pistol." She walked to the chest at the foot of the bed and opened it. She carefully pulled a top shelf out, then pushed aside clothing to uncover a pistol box. She handed it to Cecilia while she continued to root around in her wooden chest. Soon she also pulled up caps, balls, and powder.

"Here ye go, milady," Mrs. Yates said.

Cecilia looked the pistol over carefully. She checked it for signs of dirt and damp, but did not find any. The powder was dry and there was a sufficient supply of ammunition.

Mrs. Yates pulled down a worn and frayed basket from an iron hook imbedded in the wall. "This here is what I carried when I came behind the troops. I filled it with bandages and drink. We'll do the same for ye, with the pistol hidden in the bottom. That's what I done, many a time."

Cecilia laughed. "Mrs. Yates, you are a wonder. You gave the speech about staying behind, but you never did."

"No, no, I didna. And I had yur measure. I knowed ye wouldna either."

"Neither will I," said Elinor, grabbing her cloak from the head of the bed. She shook it out.

Mrs. Yates donned her regimental jacket and Cecilia, her red cape from Mrs. Willis, and the three ladies left the snug cottage for the Western Heights.

THE WOMEN ARRIVED at the copse of trees in time to hear a soldier telling the wagon driver he would lead him to the cave. As the wagon trundled forward, Cecilia laid a staying hand on Mrs. Yates' arm.

"You needn't come any farther," she whispered.

Mrs. Yates grinned. "This be the most excitement I've had since the pen'sular days. Besides, I'm an old hand at following the men."

"All right," Cecilia said. She looked at Elinor. "Are you okay to proceed?"

Elinor nodded. Cecilia squeezed her arm and led the way after the wagon.

The women followed the sound of the jangling harness and the wagon wheels, careful to stay far enough behind to not be seen. When the wagon stopped, Cecilia looked around but did not see any sign of a cave, just more scrub bushes and trees along the hillside. The cave appeared well hidden.

She motioned to the other two women that they should sit behind scrub bushes off to the side, where they could see, but not be seen. They soon saw figures carrying long crates out to the wagon.

"Can we join them now?" Elinor whispered.

Mrs. Yates shook her head no.

Cecilia had to clasp her hand over her mouth to keep from laughing as they watched Captain Melville take charge of the wagon and attempt to take charge of the soldiers, only to be thwarted by Sergeant Major Kendall.

They pulled deeper into the bushes when Kendall directed the soldiers to spread out and hide. The torch light at the cave entrance went out. It was quiet, save for nature's night sounds and the distant rumble of the heavily laden wagon as it slowly made its way down the steep hillside.

Gunshots cracked the night silence!

Shouts and crashes came from the direction the wagon had taken. Soldiers rose out from hiding places in the bushes, some running in the direction the wagon had gone. A man ran close by them. Mrs. Yates laid her hands on Cecilia and Elinor, silently telling them to remain still.

"This way, this way!" they heard the soldier softly call to other soldiers remaining. It was Private Mead. He motioned them to follow him to what at first looked like another thick stand of shrubs and trees, but he led them into a crease in the hillside.

The sound of a battle continued in the distance.

"THEY SPOTTED the wagon and have gone after it," Sergeant Major Kendall said from the tunnel entrance.

"We have no way of knowing how many men they've recruited to their efforts. To move the guns and gold quickly, they would need a gang of men," Lord Aldrich said. "Yes. I wish we knew how many there were."

"My men will show to good account," said Kendall.

"I'm sure they will," said James. "However, we don't know if they will stay together or if some will come on to the caves."

"Sergeant Major! Sergeant Major! There is a way out of this tunnel. I have brought the other soldiers through that way," young Private Mead cried, running up to Kendall. He was out of breath, but excited.

"How many are with you?"

"Five, sir, the others ran off to support the wagon."

Kendall clapped Mead on the shoulder. "Good work, soldier. We don't know if all the thieves have gone after the wagon or if some are coming to the tunnel."

"Yes, sir."

"Take up sentry positions. We need to know if any come this way. Do not engage, let them come ahead. Once they are in the tunnel, you and the men will come from that direction while we are further in the cave, and we will engage them at that point in a pincher movement."

"Yes, sir!" Mead fairly vibrated with excitement. He

turned to run back through the cave to the tunnel and the crease in the hill.

"Now we wait," James said as he stood at the cave entrance and looked out at the dark shapes of hills, bushes, and trees. The moon was lower in the sky now and scudding clouds were blowing in, obscuring the night vision they had enjoyed. He wondered what his Cecilia was doing, admittedly surprised that she had taken Mrs. Yates' little lecture to heart. The long years of being her first husband's doll sitting on a shelf for display had released in her a wild streak that both entranced and scared James. His life with Cecilia would not be dull. She believed she had bent to the commands of others for too long and the end result would have been disastrous for her if she hadn't taken a hand in her own surviving.

No, Cecilia would not be passive.

That thought plagued James, and like a plague, spread within his mind, body, and soul.

And suddenly he knew. His beloved wife was here. Somewhere. He felt sure of it in his gut. His eyes narrowed as he searched the hills and vegetation around them. Why hadn't he thought through her emotional reasoning before? He should have kept her with him.

He turned to say as much to Lord Aldrich, but the sound of horses caught his attention.

Someone was coming, and they were coming stealthily.

Using hand gestures, he signaled the approach to Kendall and Aldrich. They did not dare use torches in the cave as that would give away their presence, but just a few feet past the tunnel entrance, the cave was black. They felt their way to the back of the first part of the tunnel and waited.

"—And I'm telling you, that wagon was a ruse!" the women heard one man say as they approached the cave entrance. Cecilia recognized the person as Bishop Yarnell.

There were three men with Yarnell. They all dismounted and tied their horses to the scraggly bushes in front of the tunnel entrance.

"One wagon could not handle the weight and bulk of all the gold and weapons. It took us four trips to get it here. The gold is here, I tell you," Yarnell said.

They heard him pick up the torches stashed in the tunnel entrance. "Hold this," he told one of the men. A striker clicked against flint and a bloom of light, then another, and another turned the cave entrance to light as day.

"There should have been more torches here. Someone has been here," Yarnell said, looking around.

The men followed Yarnell as he led them to the room where the crates were stored.

"Bloody hell, they're gone!" Yarnell cried out. He turned first one way, then the other as he swung the torch to see into every corner.

The men crowded into the room.

"That damned Dunnett. I'd wager my gambling establishment he's responsible," snarled Yarnell. "No wonder he took off after that lone wagon."

Private Mead and the soldiers streamed into the cave. Yarnell turned to run deeper into the cave, but was stopped by Sergeant Major Kendall's bayonet pointed at his stomach.

The soldiers quickly disarmed Yarnell and the men with him.

"Private Mead, I'm guessing that tunnel you found connects back into the dry moat, correct?"

"Yes, sir."

"Good, we'll take this lot back through the dry moat to the bastion," Sergeant Major Kendall told his men. "This is probably the last of them; however, best to not show our hand yet. I will accompany you. I want to see this connection. We will need to notify the engineers of its existence."

Private Mead saluted and, with Sergeant Major Kendell following, marched his prisoners away.

"We still have Dunnett and Oakes to account for," James said.

"Very astute, Sir James," said Dunnett from the cave entrance. He held a lit torch in his hand. With him stood Oakes, with a pistol trained on Cecilia, Elinor, and Mrs. Yates. "We found your rear guard crawling out from under some bushes. We thought you would like to see them one last time," he said conversationally.

The women cowered close together, leaves and twigs stuck to their hair and clothing. Cecilia carried a basket over her arm. Elinor had her right arm wrapped in the folds of her cloak, and Mrs. Yates leaned heavily on her walking stick.

"Are you all right, Cecilia?" James asked, as he studied the three closely.

"Oh, James, I'm trying to be. I know you said to stay in the cottage, but Lady Aldrich and Mrs. Yates were for following and I couldn't be a—alone. I would die to be alone, I would be so frightened."

Mrs. Yates stared at Cecilia. Elinor elbowed her and slightly moved her hand in a negative motion. "Oh, Cecilia, stop it, you're always sniveling," Elinor said with disgust as she pushed Cecilia forward toward her husband.

Cecilia stumbled and fell. "Ow!" she cried out.

"Stay where you are!" Dunnett ordered James and Aldrich as they started toward Cecilia.

Cecilia made sure her cape flowed over the basket. She wrapped her hand around the butt of the pistol. She turned to look back at Elinor.

"You are always so hateful to me," she cried, nodding her head.

"What's going on?" Lord Aldrich cried out to his wife.

Dunnett laughed at them. Elinor whirled around, her knife in her hand. It caught Dunnett in the side. Cecilia fired the pistol through her cape at Oakes. It grazed the big man's shoulder as Mrs. Yates' walking stick came down on the arm holding the pistol; it skittered across the cavern floor. Dunnett shoved Elinor aside and pulled the knife out of his side. It was more caught in coat and clothes than skin. Lord Aldrich charged him, his head hitting him in the chest, throwing him backward against the cave wall. Dunnett slashed at him with the knife, but Mrs. Yates' walking stick came between him and Lord Aldrich.

"You'll not be damaging my handiwork," she cried out. The stick snapped, but the knife did not reach Aldrich.

Dunnett threw the torch he held in his other hand at them. It missed them. Elinor picked it up and swung it at Dunnett's knife hand. The torch flame burned his hand. He dropped the knife. Mrs. Yates hit his burned hand with what was left of her cane. Dunnett screamed with pain and fell back. Elinor cornered him with the torch, stabbing at him with the flaming end when he moved.

The pistol recoil had sent Cecilia backward, her head hitting the brick floor. Pain screamed in her head. As she rolled over to sit up, she saw Oakes' pistol against the wall. She threw herself toward the gun.

James and Oakes were fighting. Rolling out of the cave with their grappling. Cecilia tried to point the gun at Oakes, but with James and Oakes fighting, she couldn't get a clear shot. Mrs. Oakes picked up a spare brick from the ground and brought it down on the big man's head as he would have delivered another hit on James. He went down, blood spurting from the back of his head.

They heard more rustling from behind the bushes. James grabbed the pistol from Cecilia as he helped her to her feet. Elinor picked up her knife. They were breathing heavily, but all prepared to fight again.

The crashing through the bushes sound resolved into Sergeant Major Kendall, George Pollock, and Reuben Uttley.

Sergeant Major Kendall took in the scene before him. "I think we missed the fun."

CECILIA SAT before the fire in a private parlor at The Hound and Hare, dressed in borrowed clothes from one of the daughters of the proprietor of the inn, and dragging a borrowed comb through her pale blond, newly washed hair. It felt gloriously wonderful to be clean. And gloriously wonderful to feel the stress of the last few days leach away. She took a deep breath and closed her eyes as she rhythmically brought the comb through her hair, stroke after stroke.

She and James had managed a couple hours of sleep, enough to get them through this upcoming meeting to discuss the events of the last few days so there were no more misunderstandings. The biggest task would be to prevent anything like this happening again.

She did not open her eyes until she heard the door to the parlor open.

"Better?" James asked. He rested his hands on her shoulders and kissed the top of her head.

She lifted her head to smile up at him. "Hmm, yes."

"I have ordered breakfast. Lord and Lady Aldrich will be here shortly. As will Mr. Pollock and Captain Melville."

Cecilia screwed up her nose at hearing Melville's name, and James laughed.

"He will leave soon to report to Lord Candelstone that the gold and weapons have been recovered and are secured by the military. I'm sure Lord Castlereagh's office will see that the subsidies quickly find their way to their intended destinations."

"All I want to do is return to Summerworth Park, let Sarah fuss over me, and do domestic things like ordering new curtains and bed-hangings."

"How about letting me fuss over you?"

"Oh, that goes without saying!"

At a knock on the door, James stood up. "Come in."

Lord and Lady Aldrich entered the parlor, followed closely by the inn staff with their breakfast.

"We saw Mr. Pollock downstairs. He is waiting for Captain Melville," Lord Aldrich said.

"I am hungry and am not waiting on him," Cecilia said decisively. "Ooo—they brought hot chocolate. Would you like a cup, Elinor?"

"Yes, that would be delightful."

"I know, James, you would like coffee. And you, Lord Aldrich?"

"Coffee for me as well."

Cecilia handed him a cup. She sat back on the settle, her hands wrapped around her chocolate cup, savoring the warmth in her fingertips. "I have been thinking about Captain Melville. We need to help him."

"What?"

"Impossible!"

"Why?"

She held up one hand to still the protests. "I'll own he has made things more difficult, sometimes."

"Sometimes?" said her husband.

"I've been thinking of his situation. He has three older brothers, an older sister, and a younger sister. I'd wager he got little attention as a child. We have seen how lamentable his decisioning skills have been, but he tries. Right or wrong, he tries, and he is sincere in his trying. I think we should help him find his proper path else there will be more people unhappy with him, and he will always be miserable, but he will keep on trying because that is one thing he has learned to do," Cecilia said.

James sipped his coffee and considered her words. "There is something to what you say. Do you have an idea on his new path?"

"I have some ideas, but I would like to ask him some questions first."

"We applaud your intentions," Aldrich said. "But I can't think of any career that would suit him. He may be one of the *ton* misfits, created from too much money and no responsibilities."

She tilted her head in acknowledgement of his words. "The food is getting cold. I'm for filling my plate and not waiting on them," she said decisively. She stood up to grab a plate.

The door opened to Mr. Pollock and Captain Melville.

"You gentlemen are just in time!" Cecilia said gaily. "I was just about to devour all this food before us."

"Mr. Pollock, yesterday, how did you come to be in Dover so quickly, and at the Western Heights?" James asked after everyone had filled their plates and found places to sit.

The magistrate laughed. "I had a series of messengers yesterday, and each seemed to have more information than the last. It was like the unfolding of a story."

"I am up for a story," James said. He leaned back in his chair and crossed one leg over the other, a biscuit with jam in his hand.

"George Willis was the first of my messengers. He told me of the fire at Woodhaven Manor and how you and Lady Branstoke escaped with Lord Wheaten and his valet. Lord Wheaten was insistent that he come to Folkestone to see me. The Willises and Lord Wheaten's valet would not let him go. He is much too weak, but the only way they could calm him down was for George Willis to promise to go in his stead. When I learned what happened, I figured if Yarnell and Dunnett were brazen enough to torch Woodhaven Manor, they must be near to selling the weapons and ammunition. We had not expected that, yet. Whatever they were doing, they were not using the local smugglers."

"We?" James prodded.

Mr. Pollock's mouth pulled up in a wry smile. "I, too, am a Candelstone associate."

"What?" Cecilia set her cup down on the table with a thump, some of the chocolate sloshing out.

James turned to Aldrich. "Did you know this?"

Aldrich shook his head slowly. "It would have made it a lot easier if I had."

"And before you ask, no, I did not know Lord Aldrich was working with Candelstone either, but when Captain Melville came, demanding I turn over to him anything from Lord Aldrich, I became suspicious."

"Why didn't you give everything to Captain Melville?"

"I didn't trust him."

"That's a recurring theme," James murmured.

"I had no forewarning of him from Candelstone."

"Why would Lord Candelstone not let those who worked for him know who each other was?" Cecilia asked.

"Two reasons I can think of," Aldrich said. "With Candelstone, the first is easy. Control. Everything is about control and him being the puppet master pulling our strings. The second is practical. If one of us was caught and tortured to reveal who we worked with, we could not give our captors too much information."

"In my situation, I was *told* I would work with Candelstone. I wasn't asked if I would," Mr. Pollock said with a sigh. He rubbed his hand along the back of his neck. "I was in a difficult situation," he admitted.

He took a couple of sips of coffee. "The Home Office was more aware of our activities than I'd realized; however, as we were benefiting England, we were encouraged." He shrugged. "Mostly, Candelstone left me alone. He wasn't quite sure how to use a smuggler who was also the local magistrate until this subsidy theft occurred. I was instructed to help Lord Wheaten. Candelstone's plan was to also capture the recipients of the stolen weapons. He was more concerned with that than the gold, as he was certain the weapons would lead to a nest of traitors."

"But in truth, there was no nest of traitors wanting to aid Napoleon. There was just Yarnell and Dunnett looking for a way to cash in on the weapons. It was greed, not politics for them," said Aldrich, "as I relayed to Lord Candelstone frequently. Candelstone disagreed."

"Regardless, once George Willis came to me, I immediately set off with him to come to Dover. We hadn't come far when Stephen Moore hailed me. The young man was shaking so hard he could hardly speak. He thought you and Lady Branstoke were dead, along with Lord Wheaten and his valet. Mr. Willis and I assured him you were not dead. He broke down in tears."

"He seemed like such a nice young man. How did he get tangled up with Yarnell and Dunnett?" Cecilia asked.

"He had been sent by Mr. Tinsley to drive the wagon for them and had done so over the last four days, as he was a local and no one would have thought anything of seeing Stephen driving a wagon to Tinsley's stables. He had just arrived at Woodhaven and relayed the message to them from Mr. Tinsley that you, Sir James, and your wife had set out from The Seagull and were on your way to see me. They told him to come with them. He didn't know what he had gotten himself into when they waylaid you. He was too scared to do or say anything. He thought you were to be tied up only until they could get away with the goods from the stables. He didn't learn about the fire until he overheard Yarnell and Dunnett talk about it at the stables. While Yarnell and Dunnett went to The Seagull to wait for dark, Stephen took off to find me."

"Poor young man. We need to find a way to repay him, James, for not binding me."

"I agree."

Mr. Pollock nodded. "He's a good man. I'd not like to see him pulled down with Mr. Tinsley."

"And will Mr. Tinsley get pulled down?" Cecilia asked.

Mr. Pollock gave a bark of laughter. "Mr. Tinsley will be in serious trouble for his role in helping Yarnell and Dunnett. It was his ostlers who were with them this evening to bring the shipment to the cave. It was supposed to be my men—the local smugglers—who helped Yarnell and Dunnett. Tinsley inserted himself into their plans, convincing them to use his men—for a price. If he had stayed out of it and they used smuggler help as was originally offered, we wouldn't have had the near disasters. But I should have foreseen the possibility of problems when I learned Bernard Oakes was part of their band. He is cousin to my butler and the two do not get along. My Bernard Oakes it the one who split Yarnell's Bernard Oakes' chin. For that, he might have steered Yarnell to Tinsley."

"The last piece of the puzzle was your man, Reuben Uttley. Willis and Stephen did not know where the gold and guns would be. Stephen only drove the wagon to the Tinsley stables, not the evening run. Mr. Uttley knew you were going to the Western Heights, he just didn't know where. We went to the barracks. There we met with Sergeant Major Kendall when they brought in Yarnell."

"What about the weapons?" Cecilia asked. "Captain Melville, what happened when you drove away with that wagon full of guns?"

Captain Melville carefully set down his fork and folded his hands on the edge of the table as he looked across at Cecilia. "When the ruffians tried to attack the wagon, we fired on them, and that routed them."

Mr. Pollock nodded, "Like I said, the ostlers didn't want to have anything to do with soldiers."

"We lost one crate of guns. I pushed it out to slow them down."

"The gunfire alerted the other soldiers in the barracks. They thought the French had invaded. They organized in an amazingly short time and went out to secure the Western Heights. The one thing I hadn't expected was Yarnell and Dunnett splitting up," Pollock said. He stood up.

"Come with me, Captain Melville. We have prisoners to interrogate, and you have a report to write for Candelstone." He looked over at Aldrich. "Will you be coming as well?"

Aldrich shook his head. "As of last night, I am out of this business. I should have been a year ago, but Candelstone hung on. No more. I'm sure you and Captain Melville can handle it."

"I understand," Mr. Pollock said. He turned to the others at the table. "Ladies, gentleman, if you will excuse us, my magistrate duties call."

He left with Captain Melville.

"So, Aldrich's separation from his wife, the attack on Kate Sinclair—by the way, who tried to kill her?" James asked when the door closed behind the gentlemen.

"Yarnell," Aldrich said.

"Okay, so the attack on Miss Sinclair, capturing us, trying to kill us, and the attacks at The Western

Heights were all because Candelstone did not prevent a theft when he could, but didn't because he saw traitors and spies in every corner. He wanted to catch them all, when in actuality, there were no others to capture. There was no nefarious spy ring. It was a simple theft, like the other pint-of-ale- developed theft ideas that never happened.

"Yes," Aldrich said.

"What are we going to do about Candelstone?" James asked. "He can't be allowed to continue operating as he does."

"I will take this up with our superiors," Aldrich said.

James shook his head. "Sorry, Aldrich, but I don't think that will be enough. We need someone who will strike fear into Lord Candelstone."

Aldrich laughed. "No chance of that. You need emotions to have fear, and Candelstone has none."

One corner of Cecilia's mouth kicked up in a secret, delighted smile. "I know who we can send Candelstone's way, and he will intimidate Candelstone."

Aldrich frowned, "Other than Lord Liverpool, who would that be.?"

She turned a mischievous smile in her husband's direction. "Shall we tell him?" she asked.

James smiled. "I think it is only fair."

She looked back at Lord Aldrich. "I will send my grandfather to handle Lord Candelstone."

"Your grandfather?" Aldrich asked, confused.

Elinor laughed. "Oh, yes," she agreed. She turned to her husband. "Cecilia's grandfather is Franklin Cheney."

"Franklin Cheney? The highwayman, smuggler Cheney who is now Duke of Houghton?"

Cecilia nodded.

An arrested expression gathered in Aldrich's eyes. Then his lips quivered, and he burst into raucous laughter. Within moments, the others joined in. "Oh, I should wish to be a fly on the wall for that meeting," he said.

EPILOGUE

JUNE 1815, THE FOREIGN OFFICE, LONDON

"Excuse me, my lord. You have a visitor."

Lord Candelstone looked up from the papers on his desk. "Stafford, I don't recall any appointments this afternoon. I am not available without an appointment, you know that," he told his secretary, glaring at the young man.

The young man swallowed. "It is his Grace, the Duke of Houghton, my lord," he said hurriedly.

"The Duke of Houghton! He never comes to London."

Stafford nodded vigorously. "I know. But he is here now and quite insistent upon seeing you."

The door to the office slammed open, banging against the wall and bouncing back, caught by the large, square hand that had pushed it open. "Candelstone!" the man raged, his booming voice reverberating anger.

"Your Grace!" said Candelstone as he scrambled to his feet.

Mr. Stafford backed away from Lord Candelstone's desk. He looked from the duke to Lord Candelstone and scurried past the duke to get out of the office.

"You self-righteous, emotionless, cod's head,

numbskull, you have almost killed my granddaughter. Twice!"

Candelstone ran a hand through his hair. "Your granddaughter, Your Grace? I'm sure I'm not—"

"My granddaughter, you sapscull, Cecilia, Lady Branstoke."

Candelstone blinked. "Lady Branstoke is your granddaughter?" He'd just been reading over the final report for Lord Castlereagh and had been considering a few more revisions. He'd already had mention of the Woodhaven Manor fire removed. He didn't think mentioning the Branstokes would serve any purpose.

The duke stalked over to Candelstone's desk. "I ought to call you out," he growled.

Candelstone unconsciously took a step backward, the back of his knees hitting his chair. He fell into the chair sideways. The duke was a notorious dueler.

Houghton leaned forward, bracing his knuckles on the desk. "I ought to call you out," he repeated, "not just for what happened to my granddaughter, but from what I have learned is your way of conducting your business. You have served our enemies more than you have served this country."

"Your Grace!" protested Candelstone. "I don't understand."

The duke walked around the desk. He grabbed Candelstone by the knot of his cravat and hauled him to his feet. "I have learned that you have no respect for life, that any means to achieve *your* ends are fair means in the games you play. No general in battle has so little regard for his troops as you do." He shoved him into the bookcase behind the desk. One book fell out and hit the floor.

He released Candelstone and took a step backward.

"We are at war!" protested Candelstone.

"Yes, and you should capture the enemy that is before you, not wait until more and more come before you take action."

"We need to get them all! If we act too soon, some will get away."

"Not at the risk of our own people!"

"My people know the risks."

"But what of the others?" the duke asked silkily.

"What do you mean?"

"The woman and her son who were so burned they can no longer work and would beg on the streets if not for Mr. Edgerton. The woman killed in the hold of a ship full of women captured for sale. Those women with her, and the traumas they will live with for the rest of their lives, chained as they were in a burning vessel."

"Collateral damage. Sometimes that can't be helped."

"So, my granddaughter's death would have just been collateral damage to you?" he raged in disbelief in a voice that probably could be heard at the other end of the building.

"But she didn't die!"

"In your report to Lord Castlereagh, do you mention they were tied up and left to die when Woodhaven Manor was set on fire?"

Candelstone's eyes slid to the sheaf of papers on his desk.

Houghton turned to look at the desk and picked up the papers. "Ah, is this the report?"

Candelstone made to grab for the papers. "Those are secret!"

Houghton held them out of reach. "And you don't

think Lord Castlereagh would allow me to read this if asked?"

Candelstone glared at him.

The Duke of Houghton's eyes narrowed. Candelstone's fanaticism was indeed as great as Cecilia and Sir James described. He would see more people injured or killed to achieve his perceived ends. "It is time you retired," he said flatly.

"What?"

He laid the papers back on the desk. "I expect to hear of your retirement before the week is out. And I will quiz Lord Castlereagh about this report. If I do not hear you have been honest in your reporting and that you have retired, then you will be responsible for toppling Lord Liverpool's government. I will see that word of your debacles and near debacles are well known and that will be enough to shake the foundations of Liverpool's hold on the government."

"You wouldn't," Candelstone said, appalled.

The line of the duke's jaw hardened. "Try me," he said. He turned and strode away from Candelstone. The door bounced hard against the wall as he left.

THE TIMES

The Foreign Office has announced the retirement of Lord William Candelstone. Lord Castlereagh thanks Lord Candelstone for his years of service and wishes him well in his retirement. Lord Candelstone has not been available for comment; however, his staff have indicated Lord Candelstone's retirement decision came shortly after the successful recovery of a stolen cache of government weapons that traitors would have sold to Napoleon's agents. About the Author

ALSO BY HOLLY NEWMAN

Flowers & Thorns Series

A Grand Gesture

A Heart in Jeopardy

The Hearts Companion

Honor's Players

Regency Mysteries

The Waylaid Heart

Rarer Than Gold

More Great Reads

Gentleman's Trade

The Rocking Horse

Reckless Hearts

Perchance to Dream

A Lady Follows

ABOUT THE AUTHOR

I live in Bradenton, Florida, with my fiancé and six cats. (Yes, six. Don't ask.) We moved here two years ago after I spent 30 years in Phoenix, Arizona. I moved from one hot spot to another, but this location has rain and water.

Like many authors, I decided I wanted to write at a young age, and I filled notebook upon notebook with stories. However, in middle school, I had an English teacher tell me I did not have a writing talent, not like some of my classmates. My mother was furious, but the damage was done, my confidence was destroyed, and I stopped writing except for what I needed to write for classes.

Sometime later, after college, I started playing around with stories again. I couldn't find anything I wanted to read, so I wrote for myself. About this time, I went to a Science Fiction and Fantasy Convention with my then-boyfriend and there I met some authors.

Real live authors who were people like me!

Granted, these authors wrote Science Fiction, not Romance; however, they encouraged others to write and gave writing, plotting, and world-building workshops at Science Fiction and Fantasy conventions. As odd as it may sound, I can confidently say that I am a published author today because I learned that authors could be anybody and everybody.

If you want to write, pick up a pen or sit down at a computer and let the words come.